ENLIGHTENED:
EVALINE'S JOURNEY

LAUREN ECKHARDT

BURNING SOUL PRESS

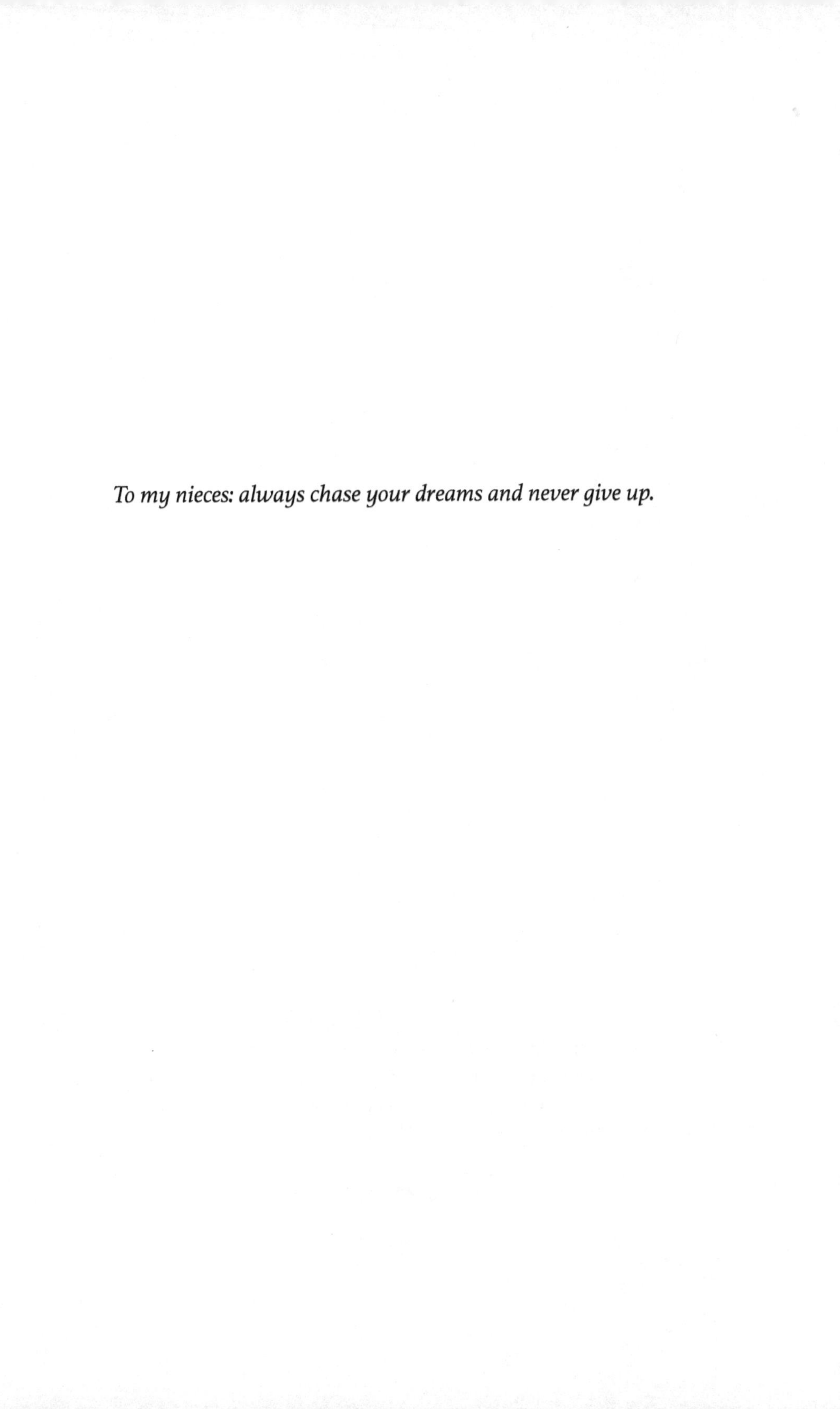

To my nieces: always chase your dreams and never give up.

ISBN-13: 978-1-950476-01-5

Second Edition

1

Fireflies

As of late, most days for Evaline were bad. Today, however, was different. It was a day anyone from a distance would have called "terrible," but those were the ones who didn't know her or what she had experienced recently. The crash brought her relief. At the bottom of that ravine, she had a different view from all the witnesses standing at the top of the cliff.

It all started with the lightning bug.

Evaline watched it floating in the air, flirting with the wind like its life was the best thing in this world. Maybe it was; perhaps Evaline wished hers was that free. When she closed her eyes, she heard a song in the background as though that's what the bug was dancing to. The music had violins and cellos- a melancholy melody created merely for the life of that one single firefly.

Evaline and the bug locked eyes as it sent a flash of light, like a coded message from a lighthouse, brightening its small circle of influence against the dusky evening sky. As it splattered on the windshield in front of her, she watched it breathe its last breath. The light remained intact, but it woefully darkened, reflecting the ending life of that little bug. The demise elicited a moment of silence from her and the entire world to honor its life.

She didn't care about the cracks that shot through the windshield instantly afterward or the way her head painfully bumped the top of the roof and window several times as the car rolled in the air. She just kept watching the poor bug, wishing she could help. They hit it, and there was nothing she could do to save it.

Evaline's eyes stayed focused on the bug's remnants long after they stopped moving. She hoped it would light up again and begin its dance as though it never stopped.

In the stillness that ensued, Evaline moved her lips, silently encouraging the firefly to breathe again. After several beats, something finally happened. While the bug did not stir, the music started once more. The firefly's song was continuing to play.

As steam rose from the engine, creating an eerie haze, flurries of light appeared in the background, moving closer to Evaline. More lightning bugs were coming. They circled around the lifeless body of the first one, swooping in and out as though solemnly bidding farewell. Then together, like an orchestrated firework show, they lit up all at once, illuminating the night sky.

It was the most beautiful sight Evaline had ever seen. Even the music was louder, filling every inch of her soul. Tears rolled down her face. She was finally part of a family, a camaraderie she had only dreamt about, faded memories she couldn't determine whether real or imaginative.

Then everything dimmed to darkness.

2

Exiting Darkness

Evaline's eyes fluttered open. Darkness. Her whole body ached. She felt as though she had climbed a hundred mountains the day before. Yesterday. She closed her eyes again. Flashes of red. Hunger, pain, betrayal, confusion, fear, loneliness, heartbreak. She could vaguely recall being consumed by those emotions but didn't know why. Most importantly, she no longer felt any of those things.

Opening her eyes, Evaline waited, hoping that her vision would adjust to the wholesome obscurity surrounding her. She put her hand inches in front of her face, wiggling her fingers, but still, she could not even see the outline.

She stood up and stretched, reaching as high to the sky (or whatever was above her) as she could, her fingers not touching anything except air. Evaline bent back down to the ground, relying heavily on her sense of touch. She searched for a sign of entry. The ground was mostly smooth with a few grainy bumps, but no holes, and nothing in her immediate reach that would indicate which way she should go.

"How do I get back to where I came from?" she whispered to the silence.

The echo of her voice responded, and the truth struck her. Evaline immediately stopped her search for a door and stood up. "Do I even want to go back?" She squeezed her eyes tightly, recalling any memories willing to surface. Colorful emotions zipped through her mind. Flashes of red. Hunger, pain, betrayal, confusion, fear, loneliness, heartbreak. Evaline's eyes opened. She took a deep breath. The message was clear: Something well-hidden deep inside did not want to go back, even if she could find the door to return.

"But what are my other options?" She exhaled loudly. "Could the unknown be worse?" Evaline shook her head in response to her own question. It seemed the unknown could only be, at cruelest, equal to the hauntings from the time before. Or there's a chance it could be better.

Better. The idea was alluring. She was more than willing to take the risk if it could mean even the slightest improvement from the unnerving flashes of red, a warning light to a path she should not return to.

Evaline took a step, trusting that there was more ground in front of her. Another step. With faith that she was on solid soil, she walked cautiously ahead- wherever ahead may take her.

She continued to wonder aloud, her voice the only solace among the void. "Should I be going in the other direction? Is it really this dark or am I losing my sight? Did I miss a sign somewhere along the way?" All of these things she knew were rhetorical questions. The answers she neither expected nor wanted. Evaline found she was strangely content.

The silence, however, was deafening in this black new world. She hummed to keep her senses aware and alert- to remind herself she's real and not stuck in some endless dream.

Evaline had to laugh at her unexpected bravery. Inside, she was trying to convince herself to be afraid, to be scared of the nothingness that surrounded her and to question her next move. But no matter how hard she tried, she could not. A hopefulness that never before existed filled her. She wanted to run or skip- but that, she was afraid to do in the dark.

After what felt like hours of blindly walking, Evaline's eyes slowly adjusted. She could now barely see the slightest bit in front of her. There was still nothing, but she could sense the darkness fade slowly into a lighter dimness. A chill ran down her spine. Her arm hairs stood to attention. Somebody was following her. Evaline couldn't see anything- but it didn't mean something couldn't see her.

"You appear lost." A voice- a real voice- that echoed for miles and enveloped her from every direction made her jump in surprise.

Evaline turned around quickly and met a blinding light. She waited until her eyes readjusted to a sight that so contrasted the darkness she had become accustomed to. Peeking through the fingers that covered her face, a shape formed in front of her: round, bold and breathtaking with rays of striking yellow hues shooting out in every direction. It was the most beautiful yet frightening image she had ever seen. And it was talking... to *her*.

"Who are you?" Evaline inquired, attempting to control the shaking in her voice.

"I am the Sun," came the resounding voice. "What are you searching for, my dear?"

Evaline looked around, hoping to see something of her surroundings now with the Sun shining on it. Still nothing; simply blackness with a lighter tone. There was no reason not to tell the Sun what was on her heart. Its light was pouring through her, making her as transparent as any level of honesty could.

"I am searching for my home. Or, maybe not my home, but a place I can call home," she corrected herself as the dark red feelings floated through her mind. "You see, Sun, I woke up with no specific memories of yesterday or the day before. But I do remember feeling pain and heartache. I don't know how I came to be here, though."

The Sun did not seem fazed by her memory loss. "What would 'home' mean to you, dear one?"

A *real* home, she thought to herself. The idea should be simple, but yet it felt elusive. Maybe she never had one. But she knew immediately what was in her heart as though many nights had been spent dreaming about one to escape what she endured. Evaline stood up as straight as she could, put her hands on her hips, and confidently replied, "A place with people who care about me and won't hurt me... one that will give me a reason I'm alive and exist." Despite her courage, her voice broke on the very last note. She couldn't avoid it.

The Sun was quiet for several minutes, attentively watching her while pondering her request. Finally, it replied, "I can help you with that. Your journey may not be easy," it gently warned. "We will tour the land, sky, and sea. Your quest for a home will be fulfilled, but it may not be in the way you expect. You must keep an open mind. Most importantly, always trust your heart to guide you."

Evaline's eyes filled with tears. The Sun was offering more than she believed she deserved. "I would be most grateful, Sun." She respectfully bowed. "Please show me the way."

"Close your eyes, dear one. Now is the time to listen to your heart. Tell me where you'd like to go."

Evaline took a deep breath, concentrating on the desires of her heart. A vague memory reminded her of a tiny colorless room that once sealed her fate, making her long for the complete opposite. "Let us go someplace green, open with fresh air. Maybe with people who have hearts similar to mine."

Although her eyes remained closed, she could sense the Sun's light fade. A whirlwind of air encircled her, sucking her in like a funnel. Despite the force, she sunk into the deepest and softest embrace. She knew for once she was safe. Exhaustion overtook her, and she fell asleep.

3

Into the Country

Evaline's eyes fluttered open. Fresh air. Her whole body ached. She felt as though she had climbed a hundred mountains the day before. Yesterday. The Sun. It gave her hope that maybe she could finally find a real home.

Thick grass caressed her body, more comfortable than any bed she had lain on. She abruptly sat up to look around. Idealistic green pastures filled with beautiful flowers of all kinds- roses, lilies, daisies, lilacs, sunflowers- surrounded her. Evaline ran to the meadow, breathing in the sweet aroma, each flower tickling her nose with a hello. She giggled as a butterfly flew out of the colorful array and landed on her shoulder. This place was heavenly.

The wind blew voices from the distance to Evaline's ears. She turned her head and walked toward them, eager to find others she could speak with. As she climbed a large hill, grunting with the pain from her aching muscles, she noticed clay buildings out yonder.

Evaline slid down the hill with the enjoyment of her newfound freedom. As she came to a sliding halt, a large sign greeted her. Brown and beaten, it appeared weathered by years of abuse and uncontrollable conditions. In a land so perfect on the outside, the wear and tear of the sign seemed out of place. She brushed off the dirt to read, "Welcome to Nogmestead: Population 2,459 and Growing!"

Several yards behind the sign was a small office labeled, "Welcome Committee." Evaline walked to it, knocking ever so lightly on the door, yet somehow strong enough to push the door open with such force that she stumbled back in surprise.

Once she regained her balance, she saw it wasn't her knock that made the door open, but rather an older woman whose head came to Evaline's knees. With curly red hair and eyes blazing with excitement, the woman ran through the doorframe. She jumped to grab Evaline's hand, shaking it with energy so fierce that Evaline thought, despite her tiny frame, she may pull her arm right out of its socket.

"Hi-I'm-Ramla-chair-of-the-welcome-committee-welcome-to-Nogmestead!" Her high-pitched voice soared, effortlessly traveling the elevated distance to Evaline's ears.

"Nice to meet you, Ramla. I am--" Evaline was quickly interrupted.

"We-know-who-you-are-the-Sun-said-to-expect-you!" Ramla tugged on Evaline's arm as she walked, urging her to keep up with the abnormally fast pace that Ramla's stumpy legs could keep. "The-Sun-spoke-of-your-desire-to-find-a-home!"

"That's right. I'm on a journey," Evaline confirmed, taking long strides to stay close to Ramla.

Ramla glanced over her shoulder and gave Evaline a big smile. "You-will-find-that-Nogmestead-is-a-beautiful-place-filled-with-everything-you-could-possibly-desire-in-one-location!" She rounded a corner as Evaline hurried her steps to make sure she didn't lose her.

As they edged the white corner of what was once a beautiful clay cottage now yellow and cracked, Evaline bumped into a flexible, wooden figure that stood only a few inches taller than Ramla.

"Watch it," the figure sneered.

"Oops- I'm so sorry!" Evaline apologized in a gasp, taken back by the menacing scowl that confronted her. The figure's eyes narrowed, fire raging inside its irises, the only containment to prevent it from erupting into flames.

"This-is-Bobblehead-Haras," Ramla introduced. "She-will-fill-you-in-about-the-town-while-I-go-look-for-places-to-suit-you!" With a quick wave of the hand, Ramla's short legs were on the move again as though she was in the race of her life. She disappeared within seconds.

Evaline considered Ramla's timing to be terrible with leaving her here out of all places. Instantly uncomfortable with Bobblehead Haras, she reset her determination with optimism that Nogmestead could be her new home.

"Hi, Bobblehead Haras, my name is Evaline," she caked her tone with sweetness and stretched out her hand.

Bobblehead Haras, however, clearly did not share the same desire for friendship. Her lips pressed tightly together and turned downward into a frown. She leaned further back, rocking on her heels, eyeing Evaline up and down once again...and over again.

Evaline eventually let her hand drop to her side when she realized Haras would not match the courtesy.

After several quiet minutes of Bobblehead Haras evaluating Evaline's faded yellow sundress and white tattered sandals, she finally declared, "You're not good enough for this town."

Although stunned by the insensitive comment, Evaline quickly regained her composure. "Can you share with me what your role is here in Nogmestead?" She trusted it wasn't a part of Ramla's welcoming committee since Bobblehead Haras had a personality contradictory to Ramla's- and not in a good way.

Bobblehead Haras sighed loudly, desiring her answer to be the conclusion to this conversation between her and this visibly out-of-place stranger. "I help people."

Evaline bit the inside of her cheek to keep from laughing. She could not imagine somebody so rude caring enough to help other people. She countered, "How do you help people?"

Another sigh escaped Bobblehead Haras's lips. Her head dipped, following her bobbing eyes like a mindless monkey imitates its zookeeper. "I help people make wise decisions. I carefully keep a tally on this spreadsheet," she held up her clipboard with a wooden arm for emphasis, "of the life details of our residents. You clearly do not understand the value of one's existence. We have an eternal obligation to look well-kept. Our residents must not wear an outfit more than once a month and not over ten times altogether. Their clothes must always be pressed. Not one hair on their heads must ever be out of place. I validate that their appearance always falls within an acceptable range to preserve the image of Nogmestead. As I said before, you outlandish being, I help everyone."

Wow, Evaline thought to herself, *how extreme*. She couldn't imagine putting such a great emphasis on external appearances. She suddenly worried whether Nogmestead could be her home. "Isn't what's inside more important?"

Bobblehead Haras cackled, her stiff body swaying back and forth in shockwaves. In Haras's mind, Evaline's words were as bizarre as her clothes.

"What if they don't pass your approval?" Evaline pointed to the clipboard, noting a red "x" as jolting as the flashes of emotions she could recall from her previous life.

"They..." a jarringly evil grin replaced the frown all too quickly on Bobblehead Haras's face, "...are punished."

Chills crept down Evaline's spine. "But if you're concerned about the looks of Nogmestead, why doesn't anyone fix the welcome sign or repaint some of these buildings?" Evaline tenderly touched the wall of the cottage next to them as paint chips tumbled to the ground.

"Don't you touch our buildings!" Bobblehead Haras roared, causing Evaline to jump. "Don't you touch anything here!"

Evaline's mouth dropped open, stunned, not expecting to be yelled at for doing something so innocent.

"You don't have the right. That building- this place- is not yours." Bobblehead Haras leaned forward, glaring at Evaline. "Things are the way they are to remind the people of this town about our history. It's special. You are not a part of our history," she pointed a long, thin finger in Evaline's face, "and you shouldn't be part of our future, either."

Evaline knew it was time to go. Steadfastly nice despite how others treated her, she composed herself and searched for the right words to end this exchange as decently as possible. "It was, er, interesting to meet you, but I should find Ramla."

As Evaline turned to leave, she took one more glance behind her, irritated by the satisfied grin on Bobblehead Haras's face. She looked victorious as though she had defeated Evaline in a great battle. Maybe she did since Evaline now questioned why the Sun brought her to Nogmestead. Clearly, inflicting doubt was part of Bobblehead Haras's goal.

"How could someone be so mean?" Evaline whispered as she aimlessly walked the nameless streets. She needed to find Ramla and ask if Bobblehead Haras spoke the truth. Evaline couldn't live in a place so focused on appearance.

As she turned the corner in what she hoped was the direction of the Welcome Committee's office, an odd scratching noise stole her attention. Evaline turned to see a fast-moving broom heading in her direction, its bristled skirt reaching far and wide as it danced along the street.

"You-must-meet-the-Town-Sweeper-Shaley!" Ramla suddenly appeared at Evaline's side. "Shaley-Shaley-Shaley!" she called out to the broom.

Town Sweeper Shaley swooshed along the road as swirling, shimmering dust illuminated her aura. She whistled a strange tune which reminded Evaline of the wind increasing in ferociousness right before a storm moves in. As Shaley glided closer, her bristles pulled tightly together. The dust around her settled to the ground, disappointed that the dance had come to a pause.

Two bright blue eyes, one on either side of the broom's handle, slowly opened with long dark brown eyelashes that flirtatiously blinked.

"Shaley-this-is-Evaline-a-potential-new-resident-of-Nogmestead!" Ramla rattled off the introduction.

"Hello," Town Sweeper Shaley's singsong voice was diplomatic, dripping with a forced innocence that made Evaline cautious. "I heard you met Bobblehead Haras."

"Word travels fast," Evaline responded, aware that if Town Sweeper Shaley already knew about her meeting with Bobblehead Haras, a close-knit connection between the two existed.

As though reading Evaline's mind, Ramla explained, "Shaley-works-with-Bobblehead-Haras-to-keep-the-town-clean!"

"To keep it clean in more ways than one," Shaley clarified, batting her eyelashes at Evaline with implied accusations.

Preoccupied with the clipboard in her hands, Ramla didn't notice Shaley's jab. Evaline was getting the feeling that the town of Nogmestead was not the most welcoming, despite Ramla's best efforts.

As they stood in awkward silence, Ramla distracted by the paperwork and Evaline avoiding Shaley's never-ceasing stare, a sight stole her breath. Out in the distance, a charming tree spanning hundreds of miles in both width and height stood alone. The green beauty was a stark contrast to the town of Nogmestead, similar to the pastures that first greeted Evaline's arrival. The outer lines were fresh, keeping a distance from the destruction of the town itself.

"Ramla, are there any homes out that way?"

Ramla matched her gaze with Evaline's finger pointed at the tree. "Oh-no-no-no-no-no," she said, faster even than her normal way of speaking. "No-that's-outside-of-Nogmestead!"

Town Sweeper Shaley shifted from side to side, fanning her bristles out as her whistling began again. They were covering something up. Evaline wondered what was hiding beyond the town lines.

"Come-come," Ramla tugged Evaline's shirt to pull her further down the street and distract her from the tree. "Let's-continue-to-find-you-the-perfect-house!"

Evaline prepared for a cordial goodbye, but as she turned her head, only dust remained from the flowing bristles of Town Sweeper

Shaley's skirt as she flew around the corner. Evaline could only assume Shaley was meeting with Bobblehead Haras to gossip about the new stranger in town.

As Evaline and Ramla continued down the street, Ramla pointed out all the businesses and stores that made up the majority of the town. At some locations, she poked her head in to say a quick hello to the owners as Evaline stood on the street, peering into the windows, searching for a hint of friendliness. Evaline questioned why the Sun would think she could be interested in a home in this town when everything was purposely adjusted to fit a smaller person. Even though the store doorways were tall, they had been filled in so that now the door would open to only half of the original height.

From her view in the street, everyone else appeared to be friendly as they chatted with Ramla. Yet if Evaline stopped moving and held her breath, the truth behind their smiles was evident. Something which should come so natural in happy places clearly forced. *Maybe they just aren't used to outsiders coming into the town, especially ones that are so different from them,* Evaline wondered as their eyes glanced nervously in her direction. She couldn't discern if they were looks of questioning or warning.

During their tour, they came across a schoolyard with children playing. The laughter echoed in the sky and Evaline couldn't help but giggle at the contagious sounds. It's the first time since she had crossed the town line in Nogmestead where there was a break in the clouds and happiness shone down.

"Ramla, they look and sound like children... but is it true that they're the same height, if not even taller than all of the adults I've seen here?" Evaline asked, in awe of the children's innocent fun, her heart filling with joy.

Ramla's permanent smile twitched, threatening to disappear, sadness briefly crossing her face. The moment was so quick one may have thought they imagined it. It was as though Evaline's observation left Ramla speechless, unable to find the right words to answer the question that would reveal more than allowed about Nogmestead.

Another chill vibrated through Evaline's body when the clouds abruptly covered the sky. The blue Nogmestead flag pole violently shook in the middle of the schoolyard. A bell rang through the air as all the kids ran inside the brick building. Ramla stood motionless.

The laughter from the children now seemed long gone, replaced with a loud continuous whirling that carried an undertone of a never-ending ring. Evaline's hair whipped in her face. As she struggled to pull it back, she could see Ramla's eyes grow bigger, focusing on a direction well over Evaline's head.

Evaline slowly turned around just to be faced by a bulky tunnel of wind that stood twenty feet above her. Resembling a tornado, it had a mixture of rain, snow, and lightning throughout. She could faintly make out the shape of a face with angst-ridden eyes. Despite the intimidating look and the strong gusts of wind, Evaline was not scared.

"Weather Raken..." Ramla surprised Evaline by speaking carefully and slowly, an ability Ramla was assumed incapable of having. She swiftly moved her eyes to the ground as her voice lowered. "This is Evaline. The Sun sent her to find a home here."

Although the wind produced by Weather Raken drowned to a near breeze, her eyes did not lose their intense stare into Evaline's. A familiar sound stole Evaline's attention as Town Sweeper Shaley hurried down the street toward them.

"I do not believe Evaline is a fit for this town. The Sun should have known better," Weather Raken spoke in a voice much feebler than Evaline was prepared to hear from an image so bold and strong.

As Shaley neared in proximity, the volume of her whistling and sweeping commotion increased. Her hips moved back and forth quicker as she danced around Weather Raken.

"But--" Ramla began, but Evaline cut her off, her intuition informing her of the impending danger.

Besides, this was the third person Evaline had met in her short time in Nogmestead that was instantly rude to her. She had no desire to stay any longer. Evidently, she would have to ask the Sun for a home elsewhere. "No, that's fine Ramla... It's a bit small for me. Beneath me, if you will." Evaline shot a look at Town Sweeper Shaley who tripped in her dance from the shock of Evaline's comment. She glared at her from the ground.

Evaline turned to Ramla, bending down to shake her hand one more time. "Thank you so much for all of your time today, though. It was truly a pleasure to meet you."

Ramla lifted her sad eyes to Evaline. "Good luck on your journey," she murmured so softly, Evaline could barely hear her.

"I trust you can find the way to The Sun yourself," Weather Raken stated matter-of-factly as if Evaline had any hope in asking for directions.

"Yes, I'll be fine." Evaline turned on her heel, walking back in the direction they came. She glanced over her shoulder one last time to witness Town Sweeper Shaley and Weather Raken surround Ramla. A heaviness settled on Evaline's heart. She hoped her visit wouldn't cause any ill-will on someone that tried so hard to be inclusive in an evidently exclusive town.

In a spur-of-the-moment decision, once she reached the cross-road of leaving the way she came from the north or retreating to the unexplored south, Evaline chose the latter. Increasing her speed to a light jog, she hoped that no one would see her sneak to the magnificent tree she caught a glimpse of earlier. She was too drawn to it to leave this town without seeing it closer, needing one bit of confirmed hope that Nogmestead truly could be as beautiful as it seemed.

Before long, the clouds darkened, and rain trickled down from the sky. Evaline passed the last building of the town, crossing a thick red line drawn on the dirt that appeared to mark the edge. As the rain picked up, her jog turned into a sprint as she aimed to find cover under the tree.

Soon the beautiful limbs and thick greenery became her protection from the storm. Although the rain was still strong outside of the tree's shield, looking up through the leaves, the Sun's rays were shining through. It was an exquisite sight, and Evaline felt the warmth of the beams through the branches. Her hair and clothes were instantly dry again. Two different worlds existed- one under the tree and the other outside of its realm.

The long, thick branches of the tree extended for miles from the trunk. Evaline could have walked for hours and never covered the full scope of the tree. She wondered for a moment if she could ask to build a home here. A secure peace blanketed her like this was the best place in the world.

Evaline suddenly gasped at the sight in front of her. A woman floated six feet above the ground with legs crossed and arms extended out. Her eyes were closed, and she was humming ever so softly. A faded blue circle enveloped her.

Evaline stood in silence, analyzing the serene look on the floating woman's face. Her crystal blue eyes abruptly opened, piercing Evaline's green eyes. A white smile beamed light as she unfolded her legs and drifted to the ground until her feet touched. Evaline sharply inhaled when she noticed the woman was actually the same height as her yet she wasn't a child. Maybe this was no longer Nogmestead.

The woman glided to Evaline with her hands held out.

"Hello, Evaline. I am Namaste Majie." She grabbed Evaline's hands with both of hers and squeezed them tightly. They were warm, like touching the Sun itself, and welcoming.

"It's very nice to meet you," Evaline's voice was thick with genuine appreciation. It was nice to have sincere acceptance from somebody after the recent continual rejections. "Wait- how did you know my name?"

Namaste Majie nodded her head, predicting Evaline would ask that exact question and said, "I hear everything that occurs in this town including everyone's thoughts. I was sending you strength to journey out to this tree as you so desired. I see it was received."

Evaline had never met someone who could read minds. She was astonished by Majie's powers and wasn't sure if she needed to say anything at all, or if it would be like an echo in Majie's mind. "I'm assuming I do not need to fill you in on the experiences I've had so far in this town then, huh?"

Namaste Majie chuckled, "Regretfully, no. I have heard it all already. But please, walk with me. Let's get to know each other more."

As they walked, Evaline recounted how she woke up and could

only vaguely sense the life she had lived before. She wasn't sure how she came to meet the Sun but found herself excited at the journey to come.

"You're in good hands," Namaste Majie confirmed. "The Sun will take care of you. You may not see its intentions at times, but all will soon become clear."

Evaline nodded, comforted by Namaste Majie's knowledge. "What is your role in Nogmestead? You aren't like anyone else I've met so far."

"It's true. I'm kept on the outskirts for a reason." Majie bent down to run her hand through the grass. "I am the town's Mediator, striving to bring peace among its people. My role requires solitude. If I live closer to them, they bicker that I'm constantly siding with one over the other simply in living day to day. If I want a freshly baked roll, I'm suddenly the baker's best friend and partial to him in any argument he's involved with."

"That's unfortunate." Evaline shook her head. "Although, I have to admit I'm not completely surprised since I didn't feel the most welcomed there."

"Well, I have someone that may help change that." Namaste Majie stood again, folded her arms, and blinked with a nod of her head.

A rustling in the trees above where they stood made Evaline's eyes widen with shock. With one foot entangled in a vine slowly lowering to the ground, a girl stood only an inch shorter than Evaline, with doe-like eyes and shoulder-length hair. Her right arm wrapped around the vine while the other gripped a book. Thick-rimmed glasses sat on her petite nose. She had a smile as authentic as Namaste Majie's.

Evaline was in awe of Majie's magical powers. "How did you... I mean... Where did she come from? How did you get her..." She was at a loss for words, convinced that Namaste Majie made her appear from thin air.

Once the girl from the vine landed on the ground, she sang, "Ta-dah!" and twirled, coming to a rest with her back leaning against

Namaste Majie. Both posed with their arms crossed against their chests. Then they erupted into unified laughter.

"Evaline, this is Bookend Rasha. She is the town's Librarian."

Evaline stuck out her hand, but Bookend Rasha wrapped her in a hug instead. "We've been waiting for you!" Rasha giddily announced.

"It's true. I confess we have practiced that entrance several times while waiting for your arrival. Regretfully, I do not have the ability to make people suddenly appear out of nowhere," Namaste Majie managed to say through fits of laughter.

Of course, Namaste Majie would have been able to predict when Evaline was on her way. They had plenty of time to get into place and prepare for Bookend Rasha's dramatic reveal. Instead of feeling gullible for believing it was magic, Evaline was moved by their efforts and preparation for her arrival. It was almost like a gift which she had never before received; people who cared enough to do something to surprise her. She joined them in their laughter, which quickly became infectious among them all as they struggled to catch their breath with happy tears rolling down their faces.

"Oh goodness, Evaline. I can't tell you the last time we've been able to laugh that hard!" Rasha pulled an orange handkerchief out of her shirt collar and dabbed her face.

"It's true. We needed your arrival more than you know," Majie nodded in agreement, her tone serious despite the playfulness only seconds before.

"But why?" Evaline asked, bewildered that her visit held so much importance to them.

Namaste Majie and Bookend Rasha exchanged subtle glances.

"Maybe we should go inside?" Rasha asked Majie.

"Yes, let's do that." Majie turned to Evaline and said, "Follow us, and we will talk more."

They strolled in silence until they stood at the base of the massive tree. The broad trunk was shiny and smooth, almost looking too perfect to be real. Evaline walked closer, running her hand along the dark brown oak as tiny flakes fell, proving that it was natural.

"This is beautiful," she whispered.

There was one single black knot on the oak, the sole blemish, which only enhanced the tree's perfection. She pushed her finger against it.

"Ding, ding, ding, ding-iling-ding-iling-ding-dong," a voice as beautiful as a nightingale's sang.

"Oh!" Evaline stumbled back in surprise as a small door in the trunk swung wide open.

Majie and Rasha both reached out to catch Evaline before she tumbled to the ground.

"Sorry! We should have warned you!" Rasha giggled.

"No, no. It was my fault- I shouldn't have touched it at all," Evaline apologized profusely, remembering the way Bobblehead Haras yelled at her earlier for touching the building.

"Don't say that," Namaste Majie corrected her. "The Sun wants you to explore all things. Do what you feel called to do. Let your heart guide you."

Evaline let the words sink in. *Do what you feel called to do.*

"Like right now. You have a question. Don't hold back. We are in a safe environment," Namaste Majie encouraged.

Evaline took a deep breath, having yet to adjust to Majie's ability to read her mind. "Please forgive me if it's rude, but I've been so curious. Why is the town built for people of average height even though the majority of the population is significantly... shorter?"

Bookend Rasha looked at Namaste Majie who closed her eyes, seemingly transported to a world far away. After several minutes of silence, the edges of her mouth turned upward into a grin. Her eyes opened, and she nodded at Bookend Rasha.

Rasha beckoned Evaline to follow her and then dodged into the tiny opening in the trunk. "This is called the Tree of Knowledge," she declared as she outstretched her arms and twirled in a circle. "It's my home."

Evaline sank down to her knees and peered in the hole, jealousy immediately filled her heart as she longed for a home exactly like this one. Cozy, comforting, and filled with what seemed like all the world's books.

"Come, come!" Bookend Rasha motioned.

Evaline ducked her head and crawled into the opening. Once inside, she inhaled deeply, her senses overloaded, her heart beating faster. "It's even more amazing than the first glance!"

Standing up, Evaline was thunderstruck by the fascinating sight before her. There were rows upon rows of books covering every inch of the circular walls. A glass tube stretched from the opening of the tree to the center of the room where a giant crystal cylinder- ten times taller than Evaline!- stood with scraps of paper and glitter floating inside. On the other side was a conveyor belt leading from the canister to an ancient mahogany desk that sailed like a large ship on the first loft. A giant ladder made out of gnarled reddish trunks reached from the floor to the second loft, which Bookend Rasha was climbing.

"What is all of this?" Evaline asked in bewilderment.

"This is the brain and heart of the Tree of Knowledge. It contains all the information of past and present from the country to the sea to the sky," Rasha called from the ladder.

Namaste Majie suddenly appeared next to Evaline. "It has become common practice for communities to erase their history, covering up past mistakes and true events to preserve an image the officials want to portray. Many people grow up never knowing the truth about the times before they existed. The Tree of Knowledge contains it all."

"So it's your job to protect all of this information?" Evaline was connecting the dots, amazed at the importance of such a position, but disheartened by the deceptive practices of community officials.

"To preserve and protect!" Bookend Rasha called down from the top of the ladder, taking pride in such a prestigious role. "Found it!" She rolled the ladder, the wheels scraping against the floor, and placed the book in the tube's opening. With a loud swoosh, it whipped through the duct straight into Namaste Majie's hands as she caught it without a blink of her eyes. The book was massive, easily reaching from Majie's knees to the top of her head.

"This is what I want you to read. It will answer your question about why the town was built for average-sized beings. It's Nogmestead's true history, revealing the evolution from a place of paradise to... well..." Namaste Majie searched for the right words to say, "...a prison." She pulled a key from the necklace she wore, unlocked the gold-coated lock on the trunk-bound-book and handed *Country Living* to Evaline. "Read page sixteen," she directed.

Evaline delicately took the book in her hands, fully aware of the importance that this one manuscript held. The weight was more significant than she anticipated and the size made it awkward to hold. Evaline spotted a chair formed out of piles of books. She made her way to the it and sat down, resting the text carefully in her lap. Taking a deep breath, she flipped to page sixteen, and read:

Nogmestead was a beautiful, green paradise that all the other lands envied. Its vegetation abundantly grew, and the water that ran through it was the purest form, overflowing with natural vitamins and minerals that gave residents everything they needed for survival.

The town was filled with the happiest people that ever existed in any of the lands. They had hearts made of gold, always serving each other and collectively serving the community as one perfectly formed entity.

However, among the goodness was a family best known for their shorter, wooden statuesque that soon overthrew the town officials: The Bobblehead Clan. The ancestors of the Bobblehead family were evil wooden gnomes filled with bitterness and resentment toward the known fact that everyone surrounding them was much taller. Focused on outward appearances, they glowered when forced to raise their heads to look up at anyone else, mistakenly categorizing one's height as a rank of being better than others. Over the centuries, as they continually sowed the Seed of Fury, their jealousy became a powerful propeller in their devious plan to control the town.

The Bobblehead Clan targeted Weather Raken, the most powerful person in Nogmestead, manipulating her to be on their side. Weather Raken knew more than anyone else about the town's environment since she was in tune with nature and understood each organism's contribution to fueling the town's food sources and beauty. Because of her valued knowledge, she was eternally instated by the Sun to determine the weather, which in turn, influenced the vegetation and daily attitudes of the town. Nogmestead's success throughout the years was heavily dependent on Weather Raken's choices, even though she was unaware of the power she held. Failing to see her worth, she felt quite lonely instead since her existence marked thousands of years with no family or friends of her own. Although the townspeople always appreciated Weather Raken, many were intimidated by her size and power, so hesitated getting too close. As with any relationship, the threat of making someone angry exists, and they didn't want to risk that since the whole town would then pay. If they were nice and kept their distance, Nogmestead would continue to receive cloudless days and only enough rain to help the plants grow.

The wicked Bobblehead Ancestors took advantage of Weather Raken's isolation by befriending her. They promised Weather Raken that she would always be one of them if she beat and battered the town with her strong winds and never-ending rains.

Weather Raken had waited many years to feel as though she was part of a family, so she listened to what she was told since her desire for inclusion overtook any rationale. Weather Raken frightened the residents in the town of Nogmestead with terrible conditions for months on end. The vegetation drowned and the green lands turned to brown.

The Bobblehead Ancestors called the town of Nogmestead together one day. "People of Nogmestead," they said in unison, "Weather Raken has been sent to batter our town because of your Evilness. You dream big dreams, and you put others before yourself. You save your money and don't spend it on treasures of the world. You are living a life for Evil, and the weather has been sent to destroy you."

Gasps rippled through the crowd. Whispers were exchanged as they struggled to understand what was being said. Suddenly, they were filled with doubt, wondering if they weren't living life as they were supposed to for all these years.

Since the people of Nogmestead were really filled with Good (and not Evil), they had pure hearts and assumed no one would lie to them. Sadly, they believed the Bobblehead Ancestors and were therefore overwhelmed with guilt, wrongly assuming they were Evil and not Good after all. They spent days crying and repenting their wrongs (that were not actually wrongs). Many became so confused, they refused to speak at all anymore.

Their perplexed struggle to understand the battle of Good and Evil and Truth and Lies became so great, that throughout the months following this confrontation, they became shorter. An ounce of confidence lost would amount to an inch they would shrink. In time, the people of Nogmestead shrank to a height of approximately two inches less than that of the Bobblehead gnomes. The Bobblehead Ancestors rejoiced at now being the tall ones. Since then, their sole intention for life has been to forever inflict inferiority upon the people of Nogmestead, so they never regain their confidence- or their height.

Evaline closed the book carefully, feeling privy to have read the truth, but fraught by the history of Nogmestead's people. As she let the knowledge soak, she asked, "So why are you two of regular height?"

Bookend Rasha had snuck down the ladder and was sitting on the floor, cross-legged while Evaline read the history. She blinked her gloomy eyes and responded, "Namaste Majie came from a line of Mediators. When you are called to the battlefield to fix conflicts between Good and Evil, you have to confidently stand up to the Evil and speak on behalf of the Good. So Namaste Majie's ancestors never lost their height. And the same goes for my ancestors. We have always known the true history of our existence and were called to guard the Tree of Knowledge and be the keeper of all its secrets. Since we know the truth, our confidence never left us. We are rooted in the fact that we come from Good and serve Good each and every day."

"However," Namaste Majie interjected, "this is why Bookend Rasha's family has been confined to the back of the town, hidden by the tree's branches. They are not allowed to be seen by the residents of Nogmestead or any other community. When she is called to bring about knowledge, she has to hide behind a curtain so that nobody can see her- they can only hear her voice."

"What about the children I saw at the schoolyard, though? They looked to be of regular child height."

"Yes," Rasha woefully confirmed. "But only until they reach the middle school years. That's when they fall victim to the lies, lose their confidence and begin to shrink like everyone else."

"Can't you help them regain their confidence, though? Show them they were right about being Good. They're not Evil people." Passion rose in Evaline since she was now a witness to the injustice taking place. "We have to rebuild Nogmestead to be all that it used to be!"

Bookend Rasha shook her head. "No, we can't. Many of them don't know this history."

Namaste Majie floated to a small window in the tree and looked out at the land through a telescope attached to the ledge. "Sweeper Shaley was appointed to sweep these stories away and create a new history soaked in lies. The chronicles shared to the townspeople today are edited to imply everyone was born like this from the beginning. The Bobblehead Clan spent decades trying to destroy the truth. We have spent the same time saving it, which is why Bookend Rasha hides here and protects the pages that document it all."

"Sweeper Shaley sweeps all the pieces of truth that escape into this tree since it cannot go anywhere else. That's the glitter you see in the cylinder, which then forms into scraps of paper until a full page or book is pieced together for shelving. Weather Raken has tried to destroy my home with earthquakes and tornadoes and fires, but it still stands strong. Not even Evil can destroy it. Good will always save," Rasha added.

Namaste Majie cleared her throat and said, "Some say Weather Raken cannot destroy the tree because a little Good still resides in her despite being brainwashed over the years by the Bobblehead Clan. This is why it rains so much here. She tries to destroy the hearts and souls of those created with Good, but then she pours tears of rain as the guilt eats away at her."

"Hmph," Bookend Rasha turned to Evaline with tears in her eyes, "Yet those that have been in her path of destruction would argue against the idea of any Good being in her at all."

They all sat in silence, individually digesting the dismal revelations. Suddenly a loud howl swooped through the tree's entryway, blowing open the door as the ground forcefully shook. Bookend Rasha ran to the entryway, slamming the door shut and locking it in place.

Namaste Majie helped push piles of books against the door. "Evaline, our time here has ended for now. You have to leave. Until we meet again." She nodded once toward Evaline before closing her eyes in concentration. Emitting an orange circle of light, her full body was swathed to look like a fireball and thrown against the door.

Evaline was baffled by the sudden drastic turn. She was enjoying her time with Majie and Rasha and wanted to help them protect the tree. She wasn't ready to leave yet!

"Hurry! Follow me!" Rasha grabbed Evaline's hand, pulling her through the maze of books to the back of the room before she could protest.

A spiral staircase hid behind one of the walls, only visible once Rasha tugged on a book to raise the faux-bookshelf tarp. Together, they sprinted up the stairs until they reached the top. Evaline panted from being out of breath, while Rasha could still run several more flights without stopping.

Bookend Rasha slid open an arched window and poked her head out. Turning around, she apologized, "I'm so sorry our visit is cut short. Weather Raken must have discovered you are here. It's not safe for you right now. Namaste Majie will keep her distracted as long as possible."

"Wait! I have to ask one thing before I go." Desperate for answers, Evaline was willing to risk her life to get them. "You and Majie both said you needed me to come here. Why? Why did you need me? I thought this journey was for me and not for others."

Frantically glancing behind her, Bookend Rasha sighed, conflicted. "A person's journey is never only about them. You will save us. Please don't ask me more. Not yet. But we simply know- you are the turning point in our story, and we've been waiting for you."

Never in a million years would Evaline have assumed that's what they meant by being happy she arrived. "Me? What? How?"

Bookend Rasha shook her head. "I already said much more than I should have. You have to go. Run to the west. You will be able to catch the Sun before it leaves to rest."

Evaline peered out of the hole in the tree. The rattling signs from buildings in Nogmestead echoed throughout the sky, adding to the eeriness. The branches of the Tree of Knowledge swooped in a symbolic dance, trying to protect them from Weather Raken's threats.

Bookend Rasha tightly embraced Evaline.

"I promise I will come back," Evaline whispered.

Bookend Rasha stepped back and gave a single nod. "Go, now. The tree will catch you. Trust it, and it will carry you."

Evaline turned to the window, ignoring the dizziness that flooded her as she looked at the looming distance between the window and the ground. She climbed over the side with her legs dangling in the wind.

She took one last glance at Rasha to receive confirmation that this is what she should be doing. Evaline wasn't sure how the tree limbs above would catch her as she fell. But, she knew these people were made of Good, and she was willing to put her faith in that.

Evaline pushed herself out of the window. Instantly, her body connected with a soft invisible slide that zipped her out from the window like a rocket. As her hips and legs sporadically bumped against the rubber-like textured sides, shocks of light identified the natural material used to create them.

"Banana leaves!" Evaline called out once she recognized them, giggling at the amazing contraption Rasha and Majie had created.

She leaned back on the slide, allowing it to take her as far as it wanted. She watched the branches and leaves in the tree above her, in wonderment of their majestic beauty as they swayed in the winds. The movement dwindled as Evaline drifted further away from Nogmestead. Soon, there was nothing but a perfectly blue sky.

The trip gave her time to meditate on Rasha's words about how Evaline would save them. Surely, she must be mistaken. Evaline couldn't save herself, so how could she save others? The Sun must be planning to bring someone else to Nogmestead soon to help them instead. Oh, how she hoped that was true. Bookend Rasha and Namaste Majie deserved paramount happiness, not to feel so dispirited in their own home.

After what felt like hours on the best ride of her life, Evaline finally came to a skidding stop in the grass. She hopped up, turned back, and searched for the slide with her hands. Not only did it turn invisible once again, but it completely disappeared. "Magic," Evaline murmured out loud. Although impressed with the trick, she found herself disappointed to no longer have a possible method of access to Rasha and Majie. Clearly, she wouldn't be the one to save them if she couldn't return. But maybe she gave them hope, a gift equal to what she received from them.

Evaluating the new landscape, Evaline wondered if she was in the middle of nowhere. An open field with no trees or plants as far as the eye could see. She already missed the majestic Tree of Knowledge.

The Sun drifted in the sky further from her, so she called out to it, "Oh, Sun!"

The Sun must have not heard because it did not stop moving. Evaline ran to it as fast as she could, but couldn't catch up. Eventually, she fell to the ground, wearied by a sad heart and aching legs.

As she watched the sky grow fainter, she thought of her new friends in Nogmestead. She never had real friends before. There had to be *something* someone could do to help them and all of those nice people in town immorally tricked by the Bobblehead Clan.

Evaline's eyes grew heavier until she could no longer keep them open. "Oh Sun, I'm ready..." As she fell asleep, she wondered if she was floating. *How strange...*

4

———————

Up in the Sky

Evaline's eyes fluttered open to a dimming sky above her. Her whole body ached as though she climbed a hundred mountains the day before. Yesterday. The Sun. It gave her hope that maybe she could finally find a home. A real home. She shuddered as the flashes of feelings from before ran through her body, nerves throbbing but stopping before they entered the brain where the memories could pass the haunting images to her mind, reminding her of what was left behind.

Bookend Rasha and Namaste Majie from Nogmestead entered Evaline's mind instead, inspiring rays of yellow to offset the crimson red swirls of times before. They could have all been good friends. Real friends are a rare treasure. It made her want to hold on to Rasha and Majie even tighter. Evaline would have been happy to live in that beautiful Tree of Knowledge with them, finding her own role that would also benefit the people in Nogmestead. She wondered if it was

29

still possible, to stay hidden from the wrath of Weather Raken, so that the people of Nogmestead didn't have to further suffer on her account. Maybe she could even save them. Somehow.

"How do I get back?" she pondered out loud. She peered at the Sun dropping lower in the sky, much too far away to chase. The Sun was in the same position as when she fell asleep, strange because now it seemed to be moving so much faster.

Evaline swiftly sat up, sensing she was someplace different than the green lands she fell asleep in. As she surveyed the sight, she noted that even though the scenery had drastically changed, she felt as though she had been here before. But if she had been, it must have only been a dream for white fluffy pillows covered everything around her. Clouds. She was no longer on the ground, but now, up in The Sky.

Giggling, Evaline whispered, "Oh, Sun, you're quite tricky, huh?" She rested on the cloud pillow, basking in the last of the Sun's warmth. She observed how its eyes missed nothing that occurred, despite its growing distance. Its rays shot out at different times in all directions to help those in need.

Evaline wondered what it was like to be in such a position where one was called on all the time and saw everything that happened. She realized then she had only counted on it to help her move forward; Evaline never asked the Sun about her past. She wondered if it knew where she came from or the reasons for the severely hurtful feelings that overwhelmed her when she tried to recall the days before she arrived in darkness.

With resolve in her mind, she stood up, preparing to ask the Sun these questions, when a shout from behind interrupted her motive.

"Ooh, it's time! Everyone, it's time!"

Evaline turned around, squinting into the cloud mists as they parted, for the first time noticing hundreds upon hundreds of people scattered behind the thin veil. Adults and children, all variations of ethnicities and races and sizes and shapes, stood side by side in a stunning visual of the world's diversity. Some held hands as others pointed to the sky, watching the blue canvas darken.

Everyone gathered around the edges of the clouds, every surface covered with beautiful bodies. Evaline trembled from the collective anticipation of the event about to take place. The excited murmuring of the crowd ceased to a hush when a dark cloak emerged. The figure distanced itself from the rest of the people and glanced at the departing Sun, who nodded and lowered itself further from its mount in the sky.

The figure stepped to the edge of its cloud, exhaled, and pushed the hood of her cloak from her head, revealing thick beautiful hair that tumbled down to the ground behind her as though it was the most magnificent train of a wedding gown. Every strand was a distinct shade of color in a painter's palette, a stark contrast from her dark brown skin which made her entire being illuminate.

Slowly, she extended her left hand with her fingers balled in a fist. She took another breath and pointed a finger straight into the sky as though heatedly accusing somebody of a wrong action. However, out of the point of her finger came a spray of radiant pink that hovered in a wavelike shape. She steadied her finger and moved it ever so slightly to set the wave with such precision that it dramatically outlined the Sun's escape beyond the horizon.

Her middle finger then shot out as quickly as the first- except this color of pink was a shade darker than the one before it. The cloaked figure angled her middle finger marginally above her index finger so that the two colors overlapped faintly, yet ever so perfectly.

She continued this process with each of her fingers on her left hand and then repeated it with the fingers on her right hand. Each extension represented various shades of oranges, reds and purples until she had a creation that would have been the most valuable of paintings if it were hanging in a museum filled with all the world's masterpieces.

The cloaked figure held her design steady until the Sun completely disappeared and the Moon replaced the Sun's watch for the night. She then abruptly closed her fist and reached behind her head, her fingers gripping the hood of her cloak, and pulled it over her head so that it covered her long hair and hid the upper half of her face.

The crowd erupted into cheers at the marvelous spectacle. They were continually stunned by the sunrises and sunsets, no matter what the cloaked artist painted. She could do no wrong. They broke into chattering groups, each speculating on the colors the cloaked artist would use to exhibit a peaceful morning and the excitement of what she would do with the boldness from the expected storm the following night.

Evaline struggled to regain feeling in her limbs. She had been standing still for so long, paralyzed with awe at the witness of such a beautiful scene in front of her, that her breathing had nearly stopped, creating a lack of blood and oxygen flowing through her body. She put one foot in front of the other, urging them to wake up. She wanted so badly to talk to the cloaked figure, but her body was not cooperating.

"Who are you?" a high-pitched voice inquired.

Evaline turned her head, looking in all directions to see where the voice came from, but could not locate the source. She continued to massage her legs to get them to move, not losing sight of the cloaked figure as she floated among the crowd.

"She asked you a question. How rude of you to not respond!" another high-pitched voice spoke, although squeakier than the first.

Again, Evaline looked around her, not seeing anyone that directed their words toward her. Most people were still talking among themselves in groups, and no one paid attention to the new arrival. She even surveyed the floor as she had learned from Nogmestead to always be aware of those smaller than her.

A loud double sigh, "Up here."

Evaline jerked her head to the sky and staggered back in surprise. Since her legs were still not moving, the stumble made her fall to her butt, cushioned by the cloud. Now sitting, she looked up and saw an outline of stars that sketched the image of a cat with two heads and a long tail that wrapped around like the coil of a snake's body. Their eyes were slanted with small noses, and although they were grinning with starry teeth that gleamed, they seemed anything but friendly.

"Maybe she's deaf," spoke one of the heads.

"If not deaf, then quite dumb," countered the other. They laughed in unison, which sounded more like a squeaky hiss. Evaline would have rather heard nails scratching against a chalkboard.

Finally finding her voice, she said, "Hello, I am Evaline."

"Oh! So you do speak- and hear!" The hiss-like laughter again.

Evaline discreetly covered her ears until it stopped. "Who are you?" she asked, wondering if she should even care to know from the questionable first impression.

"We are Jenadine, Siamese Twins of the Sky," they paused, as if expecting a grand round of applause, and then continued on, "Where do you come from and why are you here?"

"The Sun sent me here as I am on a search for my home." Aware of how things seem to work in these lands from her experience thus far, and now stronger from her time in Nogmestead, she confidently added, "Since you are of the Sky, I would have assumed it prepared you for my visit."

Snickers came from their curled lips as they glanced at each other from the side of their gleaming eyes. "The Sun speaks only of important things. It must not have cared enough about your journey," they hissed in unison.

"That is why the Sun is nowhere to be seen. If it cared, it would have stayed around instead of leaving for the night," the one on the left, who appeared to be the leader of the two, scoffed.

Evaline paused, choosing her words carefully. She was a bit distraught with this being her second land that there have been unkinder people than kind. That was not what she expected and immediately questioned if the Sun truly knew what she wanted. Then she remembered the Sun's words about how the journey may not be easy at times. That was indeed proving to be true.

"He cared enough to bring me here which is where you live. There must be something of importance."

"You are down there," one of the heads commented.

"We are up here," the other one followed.

Together they announced, "You are not where we live, stupid girl. You are below us."

Evaline wondered if she was going to feel wanted anywhere. These lands clearly were not accustomed to strangers. Instead of stooping to their level of ruthlessness, she asked, "How do I leave then?"

"By taking a running leap off any cloud into the vastness," Jenadine sneered.

One of the faded stars that outlined their tail fell and disappeared into the sky. They didn't seem to notice.

"Your star!" Evaline called out, reflectively reaching out to catch it as if she had any hope in doing so. As it dropped beneath them, she worried about how they would retrieve it.

"Your star!" they mocked, wickedly snickering. "We don't care, stupid girl."

"And if you care so much, go chase it!" the head on the left was malicious.

Evaline pulled her head back to scan the rest of the sky. There were other figures outlined in stars. A lion eating the remains of something she couldn't make out as stars fell below it. A man shooting arrows of meteors, lighting up the sky below him as screams could be heard. She knew none of these other creatures would help her. Once again, she found herself questioning why the Sun would bring her to such a horrible place that looked beautiful on the outside, but left much to be desired once in it.

There was a tap on her shoulder. Evaline turned, relieved to find the cloaked figure standing in front of her. An aura of instantaneous calmness surrounded the hood. A soothing voice from beneath the fabric commanded, "Follow me."

"Bye-bye stupid girl. Oh, how you make me want to hurl," the twins called out in a sing-song rhyme that made them laugh. Evaline felt a sting of hurt even though she knew they didn't deserve the power to make her feel that way.

Evaline did not take a last look at the Siamese Twins. She quickly fell into step with the concealed artist, keeping her eyes directly in front of her.

"You can call me FeFe," her kind voice was precisely what Evaline needed to hear right now.

"I'm Evaline. The Sun sent me on a journey to find a new home, so I'm visiting all the lands."

FeFe nodded. "I know who you are. The Sun prepared us for your arrival."

"It did? The Siamese Twins of the Sky told me the Sun did not inform you."

The cloaked figure pushed the hood of her garment away from her eyes, displaying large penetrating irises that presented every color possible all at once although separately at the same time. Evaline had to force her eyes away from her stare, feeling as though if she gazed too long into them, she would be hypnotized.

"Do not listen to Jenadine. They do not appear until the Sun is resting for fear of its power. They only come out at night, in the watchful eye of the Moon, the Protector of Darkness. If they told you anything at all, disregard it as they were all lies."

Surprised by FeFe's refreshing frankness, Evaline's face then reddened from the embarrassment of her conversation with the Siamese Twins. It affected her more than she wanted to admit. "Why does the Sun allow something so deceiving to grace its sky? In fact, all the characters in the sky were petrifying once night fell."

FeFe stopped walking. She scooped down and scrunched the clouds together, like creating a pot from clay, until she formed two seats. Resting on one, she waved her hand over the next, motioning Evaline to sit down as well. "As I'm sure you've already come to realize, the Sun is filled with Good and loves all. It is a Sun of justice, though, and believes that wrongs should be punished accordingly, but refuses to destroy its people."

From Evaline's time in Nogmestead, she realized that there will always be a history behind every land and person she meets. She knew to ask, "What's the story behind the Twins?"

A sullen look crossed FeFe's face. "The Siamese Twins were two sisters who used their life only for the good of themselves and were very careless with the hearts of people they encountered. They would befriend people only to use the facts about them as a weapon for betrayal. After too many damaged souls, the Sun declared enough on their antics so condemned them to the sky where the Goodness of the Light did not have to encounter them, only the Protector of Darkness. The Siamese Twins were made transparent so all could see through them. The Sun told Jenadine each time they lie or act maliciously, they will lose one of their stars that outline their existence."

"So they have the choice…" Evaline trailed off, thinking about the star she saw fall from Jenadine's tail, struggling to fathom why anyone would choose to be mean instead of kind.

"Yes. They can choose to follow Good and live forever or destroy themselves over time by choosing Evil." FeFe waved her hand to the sky. "Needless to say, as you personally witnessed, since the Sun first condemned them to the Sky, the number of their stars has decreased over time. But ultimately, their fate is completely in their hands."

A peculiar thought came to Evaline. "Have you ever tried to help them?"

The cloaked figure smiled knowingly at her. "Yes, I did try. Before they were condemned to the sky, I hoped to understand their hearts and create an opportunity to change their ways before it was too late." She shook her head as a wave of sorrow came over her. "Their hearts were like ice, though, and I could not break through."

"That's really sad." Evaline's heart heaved with heaviness. "And the others in the sky? Similar story?"

"Unfortunately, yes. I have realized in my time not everyone can be saved no matter how hard we try. Everyone was given free will for a reason."

"And it seems to start with choosing to be kind or unkind," Evaline added since that theme had been quite evident in her travels so far.

"You are right. No one forces another person to be unkind to another. Everyone chooses their own intentions and whether they're driven by gentleness or malice." FeFe sighed and stood up. "This is much too gloomy of a conversation and not the best way to introduce you to The Sky. Let's restart our travels. This really is a magical place."

FeFe and Evaline continued on their path. Evaline had many questions running through her mind she debated asking.

"Don't be conflicted," FeFe encouraged. "You can ask me anything."

Evaline stopped walking, her mouth agape, astonished by the powers of all that she's meeting. She wondered if FeFe was like Namaste Majie. "Can you read my thoughts?"

FeFe laughed. "No, but I can read your face. You're very expressive."

Never being told that before, Evaline questioned, "Is that a bad thing?"

Another chuckle. "No, definitely not. It's good to wear your heart so open the way you do. Although sometimes you have to be mindful that people can read you and therefore are more likely to take advantage of you- like Jenadine."

Evaline thought about everyone she's met so far in these lands. That did indeed make sense. She continued to seek FeFe's insight as she was plainly filled with wisdom. "But why?"

"People want to protect themselves. So if they can identify the ones that are more vulnerable, they will naturally prey on them. They will do what it takes to remain at the top of the so-called food chain. They call it a survival technique when it's actually a defense mechanism."

"That's disappointing." Evaline's crestfallen face reflected how she was feeling. All she wanted was to find a home and real friends, and it appeared she would have to be stronger than she originally anticipated to succeed. Apparently, this journey would not be filled with only good things as she initially expected. Instead, she'd have to learn to discern between varying levels of Good and Evil.

"But then there are others, mind you, that are willing to be the food that sustains the world. They want to take care of others and will sacrifice themselves," FeFe fortified. "As we said before, everything is a choice, Evaline. You can choose who you want to be."

Evaline thought about this theory in the context of the citizens of Nogmestead. An obvious split existed between the people who decided to be cruel like Bobblehead Haras and those that preferred to love others, even if it meant sacrificing themselves, like Bookend Rasha and Namaste Majie. And most of the natives were choosing to live compassionately even though they were duped into believing they were Evil by those who actually were.

Briefly, a red flash entered Evaline's mind carrying the deep-rooted feelings of her life before. She couldn't fully decipher the details, but a hazy glimpse into her old life appeared; one that reflected malevolent people- or maybe just one person- that did terrible things. Deep down, she knew she was the target. She decided then to be stronger. Pushing her shoulders back, she stood taller.

FeFe interrupted her thoughts, "You are here for a reason, Evaline." She waved her hands as whispers of clouds parted in front of them and other people appeared. Some groups were quietly discussing intellectual topics with their heads together, others danced among the clouds, while several individuals were engrossed in books. "We all are here for a reason. It unfolds for us all in different ways."

She clapped her hands twice, and a small cloud floated to them. FeFe easily jumped on top as though a simple step. "I'll be right back." She threw a blanket at Evaline. "Here. Just in case you want to find a spot to relax." Then she was gone in a flash.

Evaline wasn't sure what to think about FeFe's quick departure. She thought about everything she learned so far and in a surprising move, returned to the Siamese Twins.

"Ughhhhhhhhh...," the twins dramatically groaned the moment they saw her.

"Why are you still here?" the one on the right asked.

"You were supposed to jump off a cloud," the other one added, frustrated that she hadn't run away from The Sky after their remarks earlier.

Evaline smiled up at them. She took the blanket and spread it out on the cloud below her feet. Stretching her arms with a loud yawn, she subtly emphasized to Jenadine she was no longer intimidated. Maybe this could be her home after all.

"I figured I would get to know you better while I was here."

Snickering from above, "We have no desire to know you."

Evaline smiled sweetly at them. "That's a pity. Well, I don't plan to leave, and you're clearly stuck there, so we should probably make the best of this. I'll start. Have you two ever thought about splitting up your names? Like maybe one be Jen and the other be Adine?" She bit the inside of her cheek to prevent from laughing at such a trifling chat, attempting to be portrayed as a serious conversationalist by the twins.

"That's stupid," all three of them responded in unison. Evaline was fully prepared for that to be their response. She wasn't mocking them by saying it at the same time, but rather proving a point by their cruel predictability.

Jenadine was infuriated. "Only we can speak in harmony!" they roared. A star broke away from their bottom paw and coasted into the sky.

Evaline was instantly remorseful another star fell on behalf of her words instigating that reaction. "I'm sorry, I really am." It was truly a heartfelt apology, one that had never been uttered to Jenadine before. Evaline didn't want to cause anyone to disappear. Another flash of a memory from her previous life made her think maybe she knew all too well how that felt.

"It's okay--" the right head began in an unfiltered response to Evaline's genuine sorrow.

"No! You are nothing!" the one on the left snarled at Evaline, sinking her fangs in her moment of weakness. Another star in Jenadine's back arch dimmed. "You are nothing that came from nowhere. You do not deserve to walk on the ground we once stood on!" Two dull stars broke away from its left ear and drifted into nothingness.

Evaline hastily stood, pointing her finger at them. "You don't have to be like this, you know. You don't have to fade away. You can choose to be kind!"

"And be weak like you?"

"Being kind is strong. Teaming up together to put someone else down is weak and spiteful. You're bashing other people for self-validation. That's not strong; that's a lack of self-confidence."

"We could crush you," the left one warned with a hiss as three stars that served as pointed teeth fell out of her mouth.

"We shouldn't threaten anyone," the one on the right murmured, but it was loud enough for Evaline to hear, confirming she was indeed the kinder one.

"Don't you dare chastise me!" the left head screamed at the other as another star tumbled down.

"Look at what's happening to you! Is any of this worth it?" Evaline desperately wanted to reason with them- especially the more volatile one on the left. The right one automatically suffered as a result from the left, which wasn't fair. But the left one couldn't see past its own egocentric intentions.

"Don't you act like you care! No one cares! They threw us up in the sky to rot!" Another tooth-star tumbled out as the core reason for her anger was revealed.

"Why do you think they did that?" Evaline gently asked even though she knew the answer from the story FeFe shared with her. She hoped to counsel Jenadine into taking control of their actions.

"Because we threaten too many people by our perfection!" the left one growled.

"No," the one on the right corrected softly. "You know the truth."

"Don't. You. Dare. Ever. Talk. To. Me. Like. That. Again!" the left one enunciated with a fierceness so chilling that for the first time, Evaline felt scared. Several stars fell at once, leaving the left head with only one eye.

Evaline knew there wasn't much more to say, and she didn't want to cause the demise of Jenadine. She could tell, however, that the right head had better intentions and a sweeter spirit. She didn't want to give up on her but was conscientious of the need to tread lightly.

"Okay, I'm leaving now. I care enough about you- despite your fury toward me- to not be the reason for your disappearance. But just remember," she pointed directly to the head on the right. "You are still your own separate person. Your identity doesn't reside in your history. You can change your future."

"GO!" the left head screamed in a voice so merciless that even the cloud beneath Evaline's feet shook in fear.

Evaline delicately waved to the head on the right and walked away. She could only hope Jen or Adine- whichever one that head was- would realize she still had a chance to change her fate simply by choosing to be good. Jenadine could stop their vicious cycle anytime.

A cloud glided in front of Evaline. FeFe returned. "I saw your effort. Don't be disheartened. You did what you could. We can only trust every little bit helps in some way. Now come with me," she invited.

Evaline surveyed how high the cloud was hovering. Instead of letting a moment go by where she doubted her abilities, she instantly jumped and flung herself on top of the cloud.

Evaline burst into giggles while rolling on the new cloud. Although not nearly as graceful as FeFe earlier, she was able to do it and knew how to celebrate even the tiniest accomplishments.

FeFe glanced over her shoulder, smiling at Evaline's noted feat and her liberated spirit. "Hold on tight!" she warned.

The cloud whizzed through the sky with Evaline giggling uncontrollably while a new sense of complete freedom filled her. *This is what life is all about*, she thought to herself. They skimmed the tops of heads as people looked up in surprise, latching onto Evaline's infectious laughter, a beautiful melody echoing around them, falling onto ears in every land, not just The Sky.

They eventually came to a stop in a secluded area with no one else around.

Jumping off the small cloud back to a larger one, Evaline inquired, "Where are we?"

"This is my private little workspace," FeFe answered, pointing to a thin yellow line outlining a large rectangular piece in the sky, like a floating TV without a screen. "The Sun gave me this so I can practice all my designs and gather any inspiration I need."

Evaline felt special to be on this sacred ground with FeFe. "How does it work?"

"Well, there are many different ways to use it. We'll start with a fun one." She snapped her fingers at the rectangle. The yellow line brightened as the middle piece disappeared, showing nothing but the sky behind it.

A new cloud glided into the rectangle. FeFe snapped again, and the cloud's shape instantly changed.

"What is it?" FeFe asked.

Evaline looked at the cloud. Confused by the question, she glanced at FeFe. "A cloud?"

"No," FeFe whispered gently, pointing to Evaline's heart. "What do you *believe* it is?"

Evaline gazed at the cloud once again. She blinked her eyes a few times. She could make out a sharp nose that curved into a full body with two wings hugging the back and a long tail. "A dragon!" she exclaimed, the whole picture coming into focus.

FeFe laughed, "Sure! I can see that. I also see a swan. Let's try a new one." She snapped her fingers as the cloud shifted its shape again.

"A tree!" Evaline called out without thinking twice.

FeFe snapped her fingers for a new image.

"A heart! Car! Pretzel! Angel!"

Evaline immediately saw the pictures as they formed, no need to hesitate as she did with the first. Her eyes adjusted quickly. She loved this game. After several rounds, FeFe clapped her hands again, and the cloud disappeared from the rectangle.

Evaline turned around to find out why. FeFe's fists were knotted under her chin, watching Evaline with furrowed brows.

"Did I do something wrong?" she asked, worried she offended FeFe by her guesses.

FeFe grinned, easing Evaline's worry. "Not at all. The Sun was right about you."

"About what?"

"It said we were of like-souls. I understand now what it meant."

Knowing it was a great compliment, Evaline didn't ask for further clarification, although she didn't fully realize what it meant. But she knew without question it was one of the nicest things anyone could say about her.

"I want to give you something." FeFe stepped closer to Evaline. She extended her fist and slowly released her fingers, revealing a thick silver chain with a sparkling circle attached. The pendant resembled a tree trunk, with thick lines engraved, telling a story that Evaline wanted to read. It reminded her of the Tree of Knowledge.

She gasped at the beauty. The necklace was ancient and had been around for times far before Evaline was born.

"Go ahead," FeFe urged. "This is for you."

"For me?" Evaline was moved to tears, surprised that something of such deep value could be hers.

"Yes." FeFe placed the chain delicately around Evaline's neck. "It's called the Stone of Imagination."

"What does it do?"

"It captures everything in that mind of yours and allows you to use it as a visual tool. It's apparent you have been given the gift of imagination. If you think it, you can create it. The necklace gives you the ability to do that."

A lot of power in such a tiny necklace around her neck worried Evaline. "What if I use it the wrong way?"

"You won't, I'm sure. The Sun is confident too. It said it was yours if I felt it should be. After meeting you, I have no doubt this was yours long before this moment."

Evaline wrapped her fingers around the necklace, feeling the rough grooves in the inner circle. "How do I use it?"

"There are many ways. Let me show you how I do it, but you will eventually find your own." FeFe snapped her fingers twice as the rectangular box filled with a black screen. A familiar image of a green land appeared on the screen.

"Nogmestead!" Evaline cried out. "You can see it?"

FeFe nodded. "Certain people in each land have access to view the other lands. I can tune into them at any point. Nogmestead is my favorite, though, and one I use regularly for inspiration. There are good people there."

Evaline bobbed her head, her eyes glued to the screen, hoping to catch signs of Namaste Majie or Bookend Rasha. Instead, FeFe zoomed in on the schoolyard where the children were playing outside.

"What do you see?" FeFe asked.

Evaline stepped closer to the screen, paying close attention to all the details. It was easy to be distracted by the jubilant faces of the children as they played. But when the breeze increased, red swirly hair blew in the background just above the brick wall separating the playground from the town. Pointing, Evaline asked, "Can you get closer to the back, right about here?"

FeFe nodded and magnified the picture.

"Ramla!" Evaline's suspicions were validated.

Ramla sat with her back against the brick wall, eating a sandwich and discreetly watching the children as they played. Despite the smile on her face, her tear-filled eyes were cast downward, her pain apparent even from a remote screen.

No words could be found to describe how much Evaline wanted to do something- anything- to make Ramla feel better. She couldn't handle watching someone hurting, especially one who worked so hard to welcome and embrace others.

FeFe stood next to Evaline. "Sometimes there are happy moments that serve as your inspiration. Other times, you'll catch glimpses of scenes like these and desire to use your new powers to instill delight."

"What did you do when you saw this?" Evaline couldn't take her eyes off the screen despite the ache it caused her.

"For this one, I did something special that I rarely do. I faded the sky to a dark gray and sent a shooting star the distance of the horizon for Ramla to see. A rare miracle to witness. She needed that, though, and it did bring temporary joy to her day."

Evaline was grateful for FeFe's ability to bring cheer to people in distant lands. "It's such a fortunate power to have."

"It sure is. Every day I thank the Sun that this was the path outlined for me." FeFe clapped her hands twice which cleared the screen. "Now, it's your turn. What would you have done for Ramla?"

Closing her eyes, Evaline tuned in to what her heart was telling her to do, something Majie and Rasha encouraged her to do as well. As she thought about them and how she could brighten their lives, she subconsciously extended her right fist like she saw FeFe do earlier. She opened her eyes and pointed at the black screen with her finger. A yellow spray shot out, decorating the sky behind the box with squiggles.

"Oops, I missed!"

FeFe laughed. "Don't worry about it. You won't hurt anything by spreading beauty. Keep doing what you feel like you should do."

Evaline pointed her middle finger as green sprayed the screen, then purposely shot the color to the sky so it would intermingle with the yellow. She practiced with her other fingers, white, red, and blue followed, the freedom inside her bright and well represented by the display.

Evaline twirled as each color zipped out to the sky. She skipped about, rainbows exploding from her fingers like fireworks, giddy with happiness. Unbeknownst to her, onlookers stood on nearby clouds dancing and applauding as Evaline's talents painted the sky.

When finished, Evaline collapsed on the cloud, tired in a way she's never felt before. "Wow," she mumbled. "That really takes a lot out of you, huh?"

Smiling, FeFe admired her. "You learn how to use your energy differently as you do it more. It was your first painting experience, so there was no reason to hold back."

Evaline yawned, suddenly aware of how every limb was exhausted. She lay down on the cloud, physically and mentally unable to do anything else.

"The Sun will appear shortly, taking you to a new land as it travels. We will see each other again soon," FeFe whispered.

Evaline's eyes grew heavier. She didn't want to go to another land. Not yet. She liked The Sky and knew there was so much more to explore. "Thank you..." she tried to tell FeFe how indebted she was for all she learned, but sleep overtook her before she could finish. The last thought she had was that she was floating again; this time not vertically, but rather, horizontally.

5

———

Sea of Fishes

Evaline's eyes fluttered open. Blueness. She stretched, extending her limbs as far as they could go. She didn't feel sore for once. She felt carefree. The Sun. It gave her hope that maybe she could finally find what she had always wanted. She waved at it, a distorted yellow circle high above, keen eyes focused on all the lands below.

Evaline floated in the sea of blue, awestruck by the beautiful, vibrant creatures of all sizes swimming around her. She observed the organisms like a biologist, squinting to discern each detail, flouncing on such a precious chance to watch them in close proximity.

And there was so much greenery! Shocked by the picturesque rolling hills, she brushed her hand over the scattered plants, flowers, and miniature trees. It reminded her of the outskirts of Nogmestead, the areas free from centuries of destruction. The random bursts of colors- gliding hues like billows of colorful smoke- generated by the sea life as they quickly swam by in the blue waters were reminiscent of FeFe's work in The Sky. The Sea was the splendid combination of

47

both lands. Evaline was overjoyed. Perhaps there was a reason the Sun saved this land for last.

However, when the realization of where she was specifically- at the bottom of the Sea!- sunk in, panic replaced the peacefulness as she choked, coughed and struggled to breathe. She never learned how to swim but knew she needed to hold her breath, which she suddenly could not do. Dizzy, Evaline's head lightened, her vision blurred. The creatures and plants morphed into one giant, foggy image until her sight wholly darkened.

Much later, she awoke again only to discover a tall Eel with glossy brown hair and clear-rimmed glasses leaning over her, analyzing her face. He wore a long white coat with a stethoscope around his neck.

"What happened? Where am I?"

"You fainted earlier, it seems. Are you feeling any better?" the Eel asked, peering into her eyes.

"Yes, I think so." Looking around the tiny circular room, she cried out, "Where am I?" The room was so small, causing her to feel trapped, triggering a haunting memory buried deep within.

"Hmm, maybe some memory loss occurred as well."

"No, that's not the case. Well, not exactly." Evaline couldn't remember much prior to her time with the Sun but didn't want to confirm the Doctor's suspicions about memory loss. She knew it had nothing to do with the reason why she was here. "I'm on a journey, actually. The Sun sent me."

"Ah-ha! Say no more. I know all about confidentiality. The Sun has its reasons." The eel tucked his stethoscope under his white coat. "I'm Dr. Zited. You can call me Dr. Z for short."

"I'm Evaline." She suddenly became aware that she was in a hospital gown. She pulled the blue rubbery blanket closer to her chin to cover herself. "My necklace!" She grabbed at her bare chest, realizing that the pendant FeFe gave her was no longer there.

"Don't you worry. All your belongings are in this little box here." The Doctor jerked his head to the side where a grey locker perched on the wall. A large steel drain gurgled water directly under it. For the first time, Evaline noticed the water in the room that came waist high on Dr. Z and to the edge of her bed. Now it made sense why her blanket was waterproofed with rubber.

She pointed at the sight. "Am I still in the Sea? Are we at the top of it?"

Dr. Z laughed at her endearing innocence. "Nope." He chuckled again at the thought of being anywhere other than the sea's floor. What a strange world that would be. He had no desire for travel. "You are deep in The Sea, the best part of the world. We have a few rooms designated for guests who have yet to fully adjust to this scenic environment. Everything outside your door is all water."

Evaline frantically looked around the tightly closed room. "But I-I don't know how to swim!" Evaline stuttered, fearful of how she would ever be able to leave. She couldn't fathom being stuck in this tiny room for much longer but didn't know how to survive in the water either.

"You'll learn; I have no doubt- especially if the Sun sent you. It wouldn't have done that if it didn't know you could endure this land."

Evaline was comforted by that statement. She trusted the Sun and knew it was true. "So how do I do this? How can I learn to swim without having access to the surface to breathe when I need to?"

"Trust you can do anything you set out to do," Dr. Z encouraged. "Sometimes our only limits are our imagined inabilities."

Evaline nodded in agreement. She took a deep breath and reminded herself that she could handle this. Her journey so far had already proven she was stronger than she ever before considered herself to be. "Okay, let's do it."

"Already? You just woke after fainting from realizing you were here!"

"Yep, I'm ready for this." Evaline didn't want to offend the Doctor, but the longer she stayed in this claustrophobic room, the more her nerves would allow doubt to seep into her body. She'd rather have the freedom to move- no matter how panicky the water-filled environment made her feel- than to be locked up, unable to go anywhere at all. Life was about living, and she was ready for it.

Dr. Z drifted to the locker, slid a key out of his coat pocket and unlocked it. "Your items are in here, including your clothes which have been water protected by the nurses. I will bring some additional equipment to help you. Go ahead and change, and I'll be back soon."

Evaline watched as Dr. Z left the room, quickly shutting the door behind him to prevent extra water from seeping in despite the working drain in her room. Her heart fluttered at the thought of entering this land again after what just happened to her. But as the Doctor said, the Sun wouldn't have sent her here if it didn't believe she could survive. She trusted that and used it as the strength that propelled her out of bed.

Or, she attempted to get out of the bed, which she then realized was comprised of a mattress filled with water. Evaline forcefully rolled her body over the side to escape, the mattress bouncing her body like a ship in rough waters. It tossed her over the edge as her legs landed in the surprisingly warm and inviting crystal blue water.

Evaline treaded through the water until she reached the locker. Opening the door, she caught her breath when she noted how different her dress looked. The design was the same although now the material was made out of scuba rubber. The bottom of the dress now included yellow leggings of similar material. It looked like the most expensive garment she had ever worn although it was essentially, the same tattered dress.

She slid out of the hospital gown and stepped into her enhanced dress, reaching behind her to zip the back. It was a rather interesting creation, and Evaline appreciated the nurses making sure she was properly dressed to handle The Sea's environment.

The shine of the pendant caught her eye, twinkling in the canned jellyfish lights. She reached in the locker, carefully removing the necklace, turning it over in her hands to make sure it suffered no damage. Perfect. As resilient as the tree trunk it represented. She placed it over her head and tucked the pendant under her dress. The feel of it against her skin was the confirmation she needed that she had the strength to do anything she desired.

There was a knock on the door.

"Come in," Evaline called.

Dr. Z skirted around the door, closing it once again quickly behind him. He gazed at Evaline, his eyes traveling from her head to her toes. "That turned out really nice."

Evaline glanced down at her outfit nervously. "Really? I feel a bit silly."

"Well, I think you look great. But if you think you look silly, I doubt these will change your mind." He pulled out a pair of black flippers from behind his back. "Add these to your ensemble."

"Do you think I need those?" Evaline eyed the huge flippers, embarrassed by all the extra accessories that would make her stand out even more in The Sea. Then she realized how silly she was being. Her newly designed dress and these items would save her life. No one should care about how they make her look. She blushed in response for being concerned about something so petty.

Dr. Z eyed the red tint in her cheeks, mistakenly interpreting it as an effect of his legendary suaveness. He was planning to have a nurse spend the time to teach Evaline how to swim but now decided to do it himself.

Evaline sat on the bed's edge to put on the flippers, but Dr. Z offered to do it for her instead. She agreed since she was having trouble bending over in the thickened material of her reworked dress. He slowly and dramatically slid a flipper on each of her feet, making sure the fit was perfect, as though imitating Prince Charming from *Cinderella* would generate a romantic connection between them.

Once the flippers were on, Evaline stood, slapping her feet on the floor as she tried to walk. She giggled at the awkward shuffling that resulted instead as she struggled to lift her feet under the pressure of the water.

"Ok, let's practice here since the water is shallow," Dr. Z suggested. "At least you'll be able to stand if it becomes too difficult."

The outline of Evaline's pendant pushed against her chest, transferring the last ounce of confidence she needed. She took a deep breath and dived into the water, immersing her entire body.

At first, she didn't open her eyes. She floated near the top while plugging her nose. Flashes of light entered her mind, transferring her to a time she couldn't quite recall. It was as though she was a bug of some sort, soaring through the sky, dancing to a song and twirling in a light.

She was raised out of the water, coughing and sputtering.

"Are you okay?" Dr. Z held her steady, brushing her wet hair out of her face, concerned that a patient of his almost drowned.

Evaline wiped the water from her eyes. "Yes, I think I did okay, right?"

"You became motionless and scared me."

Tapping her ears to get the excess water out, Evaline pondered the feelings and thoughts that randomly crept into her mind in each of the lands she visited. She wondered if her previous life was finally returning to her consciousness.

Dr. Z noticed her distraction. "Maybe it's too soon to try this. We should re-evaluate your vitals." He was intrigued by her and selfishly liked the idea of keeping her at the hospital longer so they could continue to get to know each other.

"No, I'm good." Evaline dived into the water again before she could give it a second thought. She had learned in her journey so far that taking the leap was always the best approach to prevent any unnecessary fears from rising.

A part of her hoped the images from last time would come back so she could gain a better understanding of where she came from. As she squeezed her eyes tightly together, willing old memories to return, she had to eventually succumb to the fact that they were not going to- not by force, at least. So instead, she opened her eyes to face the challenge ahead.

Dr. Z was underwater with her this time, intently watching and monitoring her progress. "Go ahead and breathe normally," he coached, his words crystal clear and not a bit blubbered by the water.

Evaline again didn't hesitate and breathed in the water as she would the air. Water instantly shot up her nose, making her snort and her eyes fill with tears. At that moment, she could have given up and returned to the air; but she was determined to see what this land had in store for her. Apparently, it was important to the Sun that she come here, so she knew there was a reason, and didn't want to pass on such a grand opportunity. Besides, now was the time to learn with the option of air so close to her. That safety would go away once she left the room. So Evaline stayed and continued to breathe calmly.

After a few breaths, she learned just how naturally it could come. She clapped her hands to get Dr. Z's attention, pointed to her nose and pumped her fists in the air in celebration. Dr. Z applauded in return, proud of her but also quite surprised that she picked it up in such a speedily nature. He had worked with humans before, but it always took hours, if not a couple of days, for them to feel comfortable enough to venture outside. This girl's determination was inspiring.

"Cinn ubgo osyenow?" Evaline uttered, but she wasn't quite used to talking in the water.

Dr. Z smiled at her with a mouth full of teeth. "Form your words carefully and try again."

Evaline focused on her words and repeated, "Can I go outside now?" She then squealed, realizing it was yet another great triumph. Not only could she breathe in the water, but now she could speak in it as well.

Combing for an excuse to get her to stay, Dr. Z hesitated. "Sure... you can... although I'd advise giving it more time." Then while devising a plan, he added, "If you feel you're ready, though, you should check in to the TripleLeaves Hotel for the night. You'll need plenty of rest after the day you've had. There's a great restaurant next to it- very popular among our staff."

Evaline swam to him and wrapped her arms around his thin neck in a quick embrace. "Thank you so much for all your help!" She felt on top of the world (which was ironic since she was at the bottom of it). Dr. Z helped her learn how to swim and survive in The Sea. She also felt hopeful there could be more things in this land that would trigger additional memories of her past life, bringing her closer to finally understanding where she came from. Now that she knew that could happen, she would be more aware when those moments struck so she could piece them all together.

Dr. Z reached for the door, slowly turning the knob, scrambling for the right words to ask Evaline to have lunch with him without seeming too inappropriate. He had never been so nervous before to ask someone out on a date. He was known for wooing the women, second nature to him anytime he met a pretty female, regardless of species. However, at this moment with this guest of The Sea, he was at a loss for words.

Instead, he reluctantly opened the door for Evaline as she swam by and waved, eager to run into her again after his shift if she followed his recommendation to stay at TripleLeaves.

Following the exit signs, Evaline freely floated through the halls of the hospital, waving at patients as she passed them. Her happiness was contagious and she instantly brightened the faces of all who saw her.

"Hey- you! Human lady! Hey!" a gentle voice called out.

Evaline stopped swimming, bringing her feet to the ground and hands on her hips as she looked around for the source.

"Psst- over *here*." Tapping sounds were coming from the edge of the nurses' station.

Evaline cautiously swam to the clutter of white desks, wondering who would beckon her when she had yet to know anyone in this land.

"FeFe?" she gasped out loud.

It was a cloaked figure, similar in height and appearance to FeFe from The Sky. The hood covered the person's face, hiding all facial features from sight, except for brightly painted red lips that curved into a smile when Evaline mentioned FeFe.

The cloaked figure shook her head. "No," she whispered, ecstatic that Evaline had already met her cousin. "Not FeFe, but a distant relative of hers. I have an exceptional delivery for you." Thin brown fingers extended from the arm sleeve of the gray cloak. They were wrapped around a delicate gold box with colorful stones outlining the rim. The figure hopped with glee when she handed the box to Evaline, the lines underneath perfectly aligning with the lines on Evaline's palm, causing the box to glow and proving Evaline was indeed the rightful owner. "Inside is an extraordinary gem made specifically for you. You may choose anyone of The Sea you meet to be the love of your life. Once you've decided, open this box, and the gem will capture the characteristics to save for the day you're ready to marry."

"Hold on…" The figure's words sunk in, as Evaline slowly processed them. "I'm supposed to choose a sea creature to marry?" Evaline had been open to all the strange things this journey had brought so far, but couldn't fathom kissing a fish once, let alone for the rest of her life. She made a sour face with puckered lips.

A giggle escaped the cloaked figure's mouth. "Every girl chooses their love from The Sea. They aren't scary creatures forever. Once selected by a female, they resemble the being of the one that chooses them, whatever species she may be. In your case, he will be a human man."

Stunned, Evaline deduced that in this land, the Sun's purpose was for her to find a love of her very own. "Wow, okay. Thank you." She held the box close to her chest, fearful that she may drop or lose it. "Can I peek inside?"

The cloaked figure's lips turned upward into an even bigger smile. "No, sweet girl. Love will come. But there are still steps you must take first." Shuffling backward into a tiny opening in the wall, she spoke her departing words, "I have to leave now. You must remember that when choosing your love, you need to see past the creature they are in The Sea. Don't be distracted by what's on the outside, focus on their hearts. And trust *your* heart." With that, the figure disappeared into a circle of black dust. The echo of her words faintly repeated, "Trust your heart."

"Don't leave yet! What's your name?" Evaline called out but was answered with silence as the dust fell, camouflaged in the dirt floor. The secretive being reminded her of FeFe, who she then missed terribly.

A ball of white string dangled off the nurse's desk. Evaline pulled on a long strand, cutting it off with her teeth. She tied one end of the string securely around the box and the other end to her wrist, taking preventative measures to not drop something so valuable.

As Evaline pushed through the hospital doors to the outside, she was once again astonished at the beauty that existed on the seafloor. Vibrant creatures busily swam to daily activities while coral danced below them, waving and cleaning. Schools of orange fish passed by, the childlike voices excited as they pointed fins at Evaline, oohing and ahhing at seeing a human so far below in The Sea.

A fat red crab dug at the sand, the scrapping of its claws creating a steady "click-click-click" which caught Evaline's attention. She paddled to him and tapped lightly on his shoulder from behind.

The crab jumped, quickly turning, his claws chomping at the air as though ready to attack.

Evaline put up her hands in defense. "Whoa! I'm sorry to have scared you."

The crab lowered his claws and exhaled at the sight of this human girl, recognizably confused and out of place. Although not one to provide explanations, he felt sorry for her and offered one nonetheless, "It's been a rough day. We had two bad attacks today, so everyone is a little tense." He turned his back to her again and continued digging in the sand, dumping his findings in a wheelbarrow.

Contemplating whether to try someone else, Evaline tapped the crab on the shoulder for a second time. He jumped again, repeating his defensive turn with fighting claws ready to go. When he saw it was the strange girl again, he rolled his eyes.

"Do you need something?"

"I was hoping you could provide me with directions to the Triple-Leaves Hotel."

The crab sighed. "Of course you would be going there." He scooped a large pile of seaweed and layered it in the wheelbarrow. "You might as well follow me."

"You're heading there too?"

Rolling his eyes yet again, the crab replied, "Obviously." He pushed the wheelbarrow and walked, strutting in swagger-like fashion. "Right now." He called out, not caring enough to turn to make sure she heard him.

Evaline studied him as he walked, imagining him as a human boy. She blushed when she realized the crab wasn't wearing clothes. Not like he should in The Sea, but the sight made it more awkward to picture him in such a way. Amid her dreaming, she quickly realized the crab wasn't waiting for her. Either she could ask someone else for directions or follow along.

Since the crab walked on the sand, Evaline decided to walk as well. Sliding off the flippers, she quickly caught up to him and matched his long strides with hers. The crab didn't appear interested in conversing, so she stayed silent too.

After strolling along in peace for several minutes, the crab became aware of Evaline's quiet display. Out of the corner of his eye, he watched as she appeared quite content, observing the scenery and citizens of The Sea. Most of the females he had been around chatted his ear off, but she wasn't like that. She seemed introspective- similar to his own personality.

"What do people call you?" he finally gave in and asked for her name.

"Evaline," she responded, choosing not to ask him the question in return so he could guide the conversation.

Silence.

"Well, I'm Kimey."

"It's very nice to meet you, Kimey," she gave him a quick smile and continued to watch the action happening around her. The Sea was a beautiful place filled with positive energy, and she was thankful for the opportunity to experience it in such a magnificent way.

"Why are you looking for ThreeLeaves?"

Evaline thought about the shortest way to answer that question since there were still so many unknowns for why she was sent here. "It's a bit of a long story, but the first person I met recommended it. There's supposed to be a great place to eat connected to it."

"Yeah, that's my restaurant. Kimey's Red Rock Grub." Kimey stood taller, swollen with pride that Evaline had heard about the food he serves in such a short time since her arrival.

"You own it?"

"I sure do. I'm the head chef as well." Kimey contemplated which special meal he could make for Evaline to impress her with his cooking skills. She seemed to be someone that would appreciate gourmet meals, unlike many other sea females who preferred anything wrapped in algae and fried. Kimey had grown sick of making that combination throughout the years.

"What are some of your favorite--" he began to ask before interrupted by a loud alarm and flashing blue lights.

Evaline covered her ears at the sound of the shrieking sirens. "What in the world is that horrible noise?"

"We have to run! Now!" Kimey dropped the wheelbarrow's handles and grabbed Evaline's hand. Together they pushed off the ground with their feet to swim instead of walk and paddled as fast as they could.

A large, triple rock formation with red lights loomed ahead.

"There," Kimey pointed. "We just need to make it that far." Nearing the sign, Evaline read "Kimey's Red Rock Grub." They swam faster as the sirens became louder.

"My box!" Evaline cried out as she watched the string unravel from her special box and sink into the sand below them. She turned around to retrieve it.

"No!" Kimey pulled on her foot to stop her. "We will get it later!"

"I can't leave it!" She pumped her arms and kicked her legs as hard as she could, forcing Kimey to let go of her foot. Evaline quickly swam to the box, grabbed it with both hands and returned to Kimey, relying on her legs to propel her forward since she was holding tightly to the box. He tugged on her arms to pull her closer to the restaurant. Together, they slammed through the double doors which clanged loudly behind them. Once inside and protected, they leaned against the wall in relief. Kimey peered through the window, his antennas twitching to smell the air and capture details of the unfolding horror.

Evaline bent at the waist, trying to catch her breath. The unforeseen demand for action had left her unprepared to react in the water in such a way. She was still learning how to live in this environment. She gripped the tiny box, grateful she saved it, and reattached it to her wrist.

Glancing behind him, Kimey was surprised to see Evaline bent over. He dropped to the ground next to her, rubbing her back with a closed claw. "Are you okay?"

She forced a grin while panting. "Yeah, I'm fine. Just not used to treading so fast in the water yet."

Kimey felt horrible for being so aggressive, but he knew it was to save her life. "When you are able to stand, come join me at the window."

Evaline shakily stood. Kimey enclosed her hand gently in his claw and guided her to look out through the window to The Sea.

"What is it?" she inquired, searching for anything that looked dangerous.

"Wait."

A large scuffling filled the air, as the coral blew from the force of the winds. The whistling grew into distinct screams as a large net swooped in their sight. Multiple fish were caught inside the net, clinging on to the mesh cage, their bloodcurdling cries for help impossible to ignore.

"We have to help them!" Evaline ran to the door.

"Stop!" Kimey grabbed Evaline around the waist with his giant claws. "No, it's impossible. You will get yourself killed!"

Evaline struggled against Kimey's grip, but he was much too strong. She crumbled to the ground sobbing as the screams of the poor victims faded away.

Through her sniffles, she pleaded, "Why didn't you let me help them? Why would you stop me?"

"It's too dangerous, Evaline. Trust me."

"What is it? Why does that happen? Why aren't you helping them?" She couldn't stop the questions from rolling out. She had to have answers. Why wasn't anyone fighting for them? Was the bottom of The Sea too far away from the Sun's reach? Wouldn't it save them if it could?

"It's called bottom trawling. The Land of Nogmestead created this device to tap into our resources since their natural supplies are depleted. They claim it's their only remaining way to survive due to recent extreme weather affecting their food sources."

Evaline's stomach rolled with nausea. She knew what weather issues they were having and everything could be stopped by a simple command from the Bobblehead Clan. "And The Sea lets them get away with it? You sacrifice people so Nogmestead can survive?"

Kimey rubbed the back of his neck, debating how much he should share with this Guest of the Sea. He didn't want to scare her anymore. "All of the lands work together for survival. Or we once did anyhow. Communities that are closer to other parts of The Sea take great care of their portions. Unfortunately, we are the closest to Nogmestead. Over the years, they've changed. We don't know all the details. They don't touch The Sky since they can't reach it, and they know we can't touch them, but they can touch us, and they take advantage of that every day in different ways."

"Why don't you fight them? Can't you do something, anything?"

Kimey pinched his claws together to steady his anger, reminding himself that she's only asking because she cares, and not because she doubts how much The Sea cares. Exhaling, he softly responded, "Every. Single. Day. We fight for our people every, single day. Nogmestead turned each one of us into soldiers."

With tears in her eyes, Evaline apologized, "Of course, of course. I'm so sorry. I didn't mean to imply otherwise."

"The freedom of The Sea has been compromised. Some people moved out of this portion once Nogmestead started the bottom trawling. They couldn't handle the daily threats. But for many of us, this is the only home we've ever know. Our families too. We stay and fight and hope that someday, we won't have to anymore."

Evaline wanted to cover her ears to prevent from hearing anymore. She couldn't believe Nogmestead was willing to kill creatures of The Sea for their own gain. She immediately knew it was another hidden truth kept from the good townspeople. Surely if the citizens knew, they'd fight to stop it.

"Come on," Kimey coaxed as he reached for her. "I'll make you some comfort soup. Maybe you've already heard, but I'm a darn good cook." He winked to alleviate the mood.

Evaline smiled to acknowledge his effort at cheering her up. She took his claws and let him pull her up from the floor. Together, they walked to an empty table. He pulled out a chair for her. "Sit, I'll be right back." She happily sunk into the chair, grateful for some time alone to digest what occurred.

However, within seconds of Kimey walking away, a tiger shark swam to her. "Would you like something to drink?"

Evaline nodded in appreciation. "A soda would be wonderful, please."

"Great answer." He placed a soda clam in front of her, opening the shell with his teeth. "It's all I had to offer, so I hoped that's what you would say. My name is Leky, by the way."

"Hi, I'm Evaline. Someone already took my order, though, so I don't need anything else, thank you."

Leky raised an eyebrow. "Excuse me?"

"I don't need to place an order, thank you."

Leky chortled, his sharp teeth gleaming in the restaurant's light. "Oh no, I'm not a waiter. I am a manager at the TripleLeaves Hotel next door."

Evaline covered her face with her hands. "Oh my, I am so sorry- I just assumed with the soda and all." She removed her hands and peeked up at him, "It's been a long day."

"Not a big deal! I can see how it looked." Leky sat down in the chair across from her. "You know, I can't say I've ever seen anyone like you before. You're stunning. I didn't get much of a chance to take a good look at you earlier."

She reddened, as no one had ever called her pretty, let alone stunning. "Thank you," Evaline responded politely. "You saw me earlier?"

"Yeah, I was the one that found you passed out. I flung you up on my back and took you to the hospital. Apparently, the Doctor didn't share that information with you, huh?" Leky sipped his soda. "I didn't expect for him to release you so soon. He has a way of holding on to the pretty ones. But I'm relieved to see you're better now."

Flattered by his compliment, Evaline was happy to meet her rescuer, despite her emotional exhaustion. "It was sweet of you to be so concerned as to help me." She noted his light blue eyes and charming smile. He was reasonably attractive- for a shark. Maybe there was a reason he was the one that found her earlier. The Sun could have set it up this way- like a meet-cute.

"So it wasn't just a fake damsel in distress call? That's too bad." Leky raised his eyebrows at her, causing Evaline to blush again. She could never recall this many instances in one day where her face became so hot from the flirtatious comments of others.

Her stomach rumbled in the silence, making her aware of how hungry she suddenly felt. This was new- she never once felt the need to eat in any of the other lands.

"You said someone is getting you something to eat, right?"

Evaline realized Leky heard her stomach growl and her face flushed from embarrassment. He was causing her to turn all shades of red. "I didn't think I would be this hungry after... some of the things I've seen today."

"Hunger sure has a way of sneaking up on someone." Leky chomped in the air reflexively. "I suppose I should get something to eat as well. It's been a few minutes since my last meal. What did you order?"

"I think Kimey is making me soup."

Leky took another swig of his soda. "Oh, you're a friend of Kimey's, huh?"

Evaline shrugged. "I suppose you could say that. We met today for the first time. You know him? Oh, of course you do with the hotel and restaurant being connected."

"Yeah, we're buddies. It's a small area of The Sea here, so most people know each other. Speaking of..." Leky trailed off as Dr. Z slid through the doors as though he had been running a race, obviously in a rush to get there.

Dr. Z licked his hands and patted down his hair. "Well, hello, Evaline. I didn't expect to see you here," he lied as he moved swiftly to their table, taking the seat right next to her. "Leky," he nodded to him, acknowledging his presence.

"Hmm, funny seeing you here," Leky commented with heavy bitterness. "First time I've seen you without any nurses hanging on your arm, though. Hardly recognized you."

Dr. Z ignored his jab and turned to Evaline. "Are you feeling better? You look a little red."

"Yeah, I think once I get some food in my stomach, I'll be fine." She hid the fact that Leky had been the reason behind her face color.

Evaline took a moment to glance at Dr. Z and scrutinize him in a new light now that she was given the mission of looking for love while she was here. His white coat was off, so she was able to see that he had strong lean muscles throughout his body. She had to remind herself, though, that choosing love was more about each one's heart and not what they may look like in human form.

"So what part of the sky did you fall from, angel? I mean, Evaline?" Leky placed a fin on one of her hands and leaned in closer to suggest they were still in a private conversation, even with Dr. Z's arrival.

Biting her bottom lip to keep from melting from Leky's enticing advances, she answered, "I actually don't remember where I came from. I don't remember much of the past."

"That's what I was scared of," Dr. Z pushed through Leky to look directly into Evaline's eyes, searching for signs of trauma. "You must have hit something when you entered The Sea."

"No, no," Evaline giggled. "That's sweet of you to be so concerned. But I've been on a journey with the Sun for a while now. I couldn't remember my past even before I came here."

"Hmm," Dr. Z didn't like the way that sounded. "Was it trauma-induced then?"

His question hit Evaline like a cannonball in her stomach. She sucked in her breath and closed her eyes, remembering loud sounds and metal pieces ricocheting off a cliff. It was dark. She wasn't alone.

She begged her mind to release more, but it remained quiet. Opening her eyes again, she exhaled loudly. "I don't know," she finally answered. "Maybe. Pieces of memories from my past keep appearing. I'm collecting them, hoping to form a puzzle."

Leky snorted. Surprised by his insensitivity, Evaline removed her hand from under his fin and crossed her arms, keeping every body part to herself.

Putting his fins up in the air, Leky apologized, "That was bad timing, sorry. It's only that I'd be okay with that if I were you. I'd forget my past in a heartbeat if I could. It wasn't the best." Leky shuddered at the thought of his bullied history in grade school. Now he was a confident and successful shark, and would never look back to how his life once was.

"You'd be willing to forget every single great memory just so you could let go of a few bad ones?" Evaline challenged. "Times with family? Times with friends? Times of succeeding and overcoming obstacles?"

"But the bad memories can bring heavier feelings to mind than what the great memories can make up for sometimes." Leky had a faraway look in his eyes.

She couldn't argue with that. Then she remembered her days once were bad. Terrible, long days... Evaline tightly squeezed her eyes again, but the memories faded just as quickly as they surfaced. "If we didn't have bad moments, we wouldn't appreciate the good ones," she muttered wistfully, more for her mind than for anyone else sitting at the table with her.

A pungent garlic aroma filled Evaline's nose. Leky's nose was already sniffing the air. Dr. Z salivated. Her stomach growled louder in reaction, but this time she didn't care who heard. Kimey walked out of the kitchen, and she had to refrain from tackling him. He was holding a bowl of creamy white soup with steam rising out of the top, which carried the delicious scent faster to her nose and tantalized her taste buds. He placed the bowl proudly in front of her. "Bon-Appetite!"

Evaline noted there wasn't any silverware but was too hungry to wait any longer. She picked up the hot bowl with her hands and slurped the delicious broth until most of it was gone. She only stopped to catch her breath which is when she noticed every single male at the table was staring.

Dr. Z held out a napkin, and she thought for a brief moment a look of disgust crossed his face. She grabbed the napkin and tenderly patted her mouth with it. "Wow, Kimey, you are an amazing cook! This may be the best thing I've ever eaten." She could barely get the last word out of her mouth before she guzzled the broth again, not finishing until the bowl was dry. She was hungrier than she thought.

At first, she didn't perceive the tension in the room and had blocked out the strained glares that Kimey, Leky, and Dr. Z all passed to each other. In her temporary mental absence, as she absorbed every single drop of the soup in a heavenly utopia, she ignored all the words that were darting out of the mouths of those around her, even though they were all aimed to convince Evaline one sea creature was better than the other.

When she finished her food and leaned back in the chair, her stomach officially full and happy again, only then did she become aware of the scene in front of her.

"You don't care what she looks like as long as she's female!" Kimey pointed a claw at Dr. Z.

"Like you can talk! You don't care who she is as long as she loves your food!" Leky retorted.

"You seriously want to jump in this, Leky? You don't care at all because no girl will ever be like your ex-girlfriend who you still haven't gotten over!"

"This one is different!"

"For now maybe! What about tomorrow?"

"Oh c'mon- everyone knows you have a flavor of the week."

Evaline felt dizzy. She lost track of who was saying what. She couldn't believe these three were yelling at each other, two with fists balled up at their sides as though ready to fight.

"Hey! Is this really necessary? Is this what you do all the time?

Argue over girls?" Evaline could sense it wasn't the first time this conversation had taken place.

Her comment went unnoticed by all except Leky. "Shh!" he snarled. "Kimey and Z, stop! Evaline is right. She doesn't need our childish banter. She's had a rough day."

Finally, all eyes were back on her instead of throwing daggers at each other. Evaline exhaled, wondering if she would finally have a moment to enjoy The Sea. Every potential peaceful moment so far had been disturbed.

"Sorry, Evaline. Would you like some more soup? Or maybe try something else off the menu? I'm happy to make you anything you want." Kimey hoped he could get her to stay longer.

Evaline felt full but didn't mind the idea of trying more of Kimey's yummy creations. He was a great chef and definitely knew what he was called to do. Evaline wondered if she would ever know her purpose in life like that.

"Or maybe you'd prefer to stroll The Sea with me? I'd love to show you around and tell you all about our home. I can also give you more swimming tips," Dr. Z offered. Evaline knew she would enjoy learning more about this land since it was the most mysterious one. It seemed bigger than Nogmestead and The Sky combined.

Leky interjected, "Didn't you tell her already that she needed to rest?" Turning to Evaline, he said, "I'll help you get settled in the most luxurious room TripleLeaves has with a full in-room hot springs tub and all. You'll love it." A nice hot dip and sleep also sounded appealing to Evaline. It had been an exhausting day.

As all three stared at her, waiting for her to choose, she realized she was already drained in this quest for love. If she had encountered each one individually, she would have been more open to explore what each creature had to offer. But seeing them interact harshly with each other, competing for a prize they didn't know much about, was an instant affection repellent.

All day Evaline experienced emotions she wasn't accustomed to. She had yet to fully comprehend the idea of picking a potential life-long suitor. It was overwhelming since she never before considered she could be loved in that way. Some of the feelings encouraged her to continue to be around these potential suitors, yet others told her to run. As she became besieged with pressure, the latter choice held the most appeal.

"I'm sorry- I have to... I need to go." She made up her mind and jumped up from the chair, ran to the door and pushed herself out into the open sea.

Evaline leaned against the outside wall, letting the fresh sea air clear her nostrils. She peeked through the window, half expecting one of them to chase after her. But instead, they remained at the table, in silence, drinks in hands.

In previous lands, she encountered people who were merely mean to her; it was black and white as to who was kind and who was mean. But in this land, she had to be more discerning even with those that were nice to her. Something didn't quite feel right about it. It was as though there were underlying intentions with everything they said. Even though they made it seem her best interest was in the forefront of their minds, she knew better.

Evaline found an empty alleyway and sat down on the sand. She couldn't handle another sea creature today. She removed the tie around her wrist and from the box. "What am I supposed to do if I don't want to choose anyone?" she spoke openly to the box, wondering if the Sun could hear her words too.

A seahorse floated by the alley entrance, glancing at Evaline before disappearing. Then it came around the corner again once it registered that a strange human girl was sitting in an alley alone talking to herself. "Hi there, can I help you? Are you lost?" He slowly drifted to her, almost as unsure of her as Evaline was of him.

Conflicted with emotions, Evaline was saddened by the fact that she had yet to make a lasting connection with anyone in The Sea. Except for the cloaked figure, the shortest interaction with anyone so far in this new land. There were so many fishes in the sea, and yet the first three she met seemed inclined to get to know her for all the wrong reasons.

"Is this land full of male fishes?"

The seahorse knowingly gave a thin-lipped smile. "Are we over-whelming you?"

"Yes!" Evaline blurted, then covered her mouth quickly. "I'm sorry. It's strange feeling pressured to like someone just because they like me. I'm tired and didn't expect to be so bombarded by The Sea."

"If it makes you feel any better, this is only one tiny part of The Sea. There are ones like you in other places."

Knowing this seahorse probably wasn't the right one to direct her question to, Evaline, desperate for answers, asked anyhow, "Why would the Sun put me in this area of The Sea then?"

"Most people are sent here when it's time to find their true love."

"But all I asked for was a home. That's all I wanted. Security."

The seahorse studied Evaline before responding, "Doesn't love fill a home? Isn't it important to share this beautiful life with others?"

"Sure, but why can't that be in the form of friends? Why do I have to search for my one true love?"

Grinning, the seahorse tapped his forehead and answered, "Maybe that's what you're supposed to figure out here. Learn how to separate the temptations and distractions from what you really desire. If you only want friends and a home, there's nothing wrong with that. The Sun's ways aren't always clear, but the one thing you can count on is that it knows when certain paths are supposed to be a part of your journey."

"You may be the first person I've met here that I like." Embar-rassed by her honest response, Evaline explained, "I don't mean in *that* way. I mean, maybe in that way. I don't know yet. But I just mean as friends." She knew she said too much and didn't know how to take her words back.

The seahorse stuck out his hand. "I'm Cink. And please, don't explain yourself. I'm flattered to meet a new friend."

Evaline reached out and shook his hand, a warmness filling her body. "I'm Evaline. Thank you, Cink, for helping me work through the chaos in my mind. It's been quite a journey so far."

"Listen, I know the idea of love is ingrained in us early, and although great at a certain point in life, sometimes the best part of the journey is figuring out who you are, what you want to become, and accomplishing your goals. Then when you've found you, you can find someone else."

Evaline smiled, relieved to hear someone confirm the thoughts that swirled in her head. "I was just thinking that I don't even completely know who I am yet, so how am I supposed to find someone to love?"

Cink smiled. "We appear to be on the same wavelength." He pointed to the stone-covered cube resting by her legs. "Now can I finally ask about this mysterious box?"

Handing it to Cink, instantly knowing she could trust him with something so valuable, she answered, "Apparently it's a gift from the Sun. When I decide who I would like to someday marry, it's supposed to capture those qualities to be saved for the future."

"Hmm," Cink rotated the box in his hands, admiring the gemstones. "That doesn't necessarily mean you have to decide now, right? Couldn't you someday return to The Sea when you feel more ready to make such a life-altering decision?"

Evaline felt momentarily foolish that she had yet to consider that. She assumed the Sun's intentions were for her to complete the task before she could continue on the rest of her journey. But maybe, it was simply to discover more of who she was meant to be.

"Cink, you're a genius."

He chuckled, his body bobbing with the motion. "I don't know about that. I just believe in living life to the fullest with the confidence of knowing who you are."

Suddenly, the alarms blared again. Cink's eyes closed with agony. "Stay in the alley," he commanded. "The net can't get you here."

"How often do they do this?" Evaline's eyes blurred from tears, the screams from before resounding in her ears.

"Today has been an especially bad day. We keep wondering if they're looking for something specific. But yet they're not throwing anyone back in The Sea, even if it's not who they want."

Terror gripped Evaline's heart. She knew the truth. Today's increased bottom trawling attempts wasn't a coincidence. They were searching for her. They couldn't touch her in The Sky, but they could capture her in The Sea.

"Cink, I have to go. I hope we meet again someday." She gripped both of his hands with hers before running out of the alley."

"Evaline! Don't! It's dangerous! And I have your box!"

She paused quickly enough to give Cink one last smile for now. "I know you'll protect it."

The giant net swooped in, and she jumped in its path, holding tightly to the knitted knots, the rough sprays of water knocking her in the face as though she was whitewater rafting. As other sea creatures were captured, she crawled to them, like a spider navigating its web, freeing those the Bobblehead Clan didn't aim to seize. Those victims were only bonuses in the Clan's deceptive plans. But no one else would suffer; Evaline was determined. She didn't know how she was going to do it, but she would save the good townspeople in Nogmestead and prevent the Bobblehead Clan from capturing anyone else from The Sea. And she was determined to succeed.

As the net rose to the surface, the quick changes in air pressure made Evaline struggle to find her breath. She saw the Sun fading above and hoped it would see her emerge from the water. She tried to call out but fell into a tranquil sleep before the words could leave her mouth. She dreamt she was spinning in the middle of Weather Raken's tornado.

6
____

Somewhere In-Between

Evaline's eyes fluttered open. Blankness. Her whole body felt light and pleasant. She looked around but could not see a thing. This time, though, it wasn't dark, but simply... white. Not even the Sun was present.

She jumped to her feet, recalling her ascent on the net, prepared to face the Bobblehead Clan and save Nogmestead. Adrenaline pumped through her body.

But this... void... wasn't what she expected.

Several moments passed as Evaline tapped into each of her senses, searching for understanding. Her eyes couldn't see anything; her ears couldn't hear anything; there was nothing for her to smell; nothing for her to feel; and definitely nothing to taste.

So she did the only thing she could think of and called out, "Sun, oh--" Evaline stopped short as a gigantic black squiggly mark rushed past her head, causing her to duck. It pressed itself up against what appeared to be a massive wall in the whiteness's midst. She floated to it, surprised that her feet never touched the ground. Additional squiggly lines came even faster from behind. Eventually, they formed words that read: "Sun, oh-"

Evaline stared at the wall in disbelief. She saw movement out of one eye and pivoted to her right. A mirror reflected her image as the Sun drifted behind her.

Evaline looked to her left and saw more words form on the wall. It read, "The Sun drifted closer and enveloped me in its light." The written words were describing the images in the mirror in real time.

The deep voice behind her spoke, "Your job is to be the Writer."

Turning around, Evaline looked into the face of the Sun. It continued, "You have been given the gift of imagination to create the home you seek and worlds for others to enjoy. You can make your life be anything you choose while impacting the lives of others."

The words embedded themselves in Evaline's mind and heart. She turned to the wall and saw those exact words appear in a storyline format. But she couldn't focus on that. Not yet. She had a mission to do.

"Sun, I am so grateful for such an incredible gift. But I need to get to Nogmestead. They are in trouble. The Sea is in trouble. I have to save them. *We* need to save them all."

The Sun inched closer, extending a calming ray to warm her shoulders. "You are a brave soul. Your willingness to risk your life is admirable, dear one. You need to live that exact life with your words. Be bold, be brave, do not hold back."

"But, Sun," Evaline tried to control the whine in her voice. How could someone who sees everything not understand the dire importance of Evaline saving the creatures in The Sea and restoring Good in Nogmestead? This entire journey had taught her she can live out the desires of her heart. Even Namaste Majie and Bookend Rasha said she would save them. So why was the Sun stopping her?

"There are times that you will be called in action to save others. This is not one of those times. I promise my hand is steady and my decisions are intentional. Your fierce readiness speaks volumes. This part of your journey isn't to save through actions, but only through words."

Evaline steadied her breathing. She had to trust the Sun. Trust was something that never came easily to her in the past; she could sense this to be true. The Sun was her guide in her journey; there was no reason to doubt. It could see her path from the beginning to the end. All she could see was the moment in front of her.

That's when the words on the wall finally clicked with her. She knew now, not only her purpose, but her most potent weapon in combating the Evil that existed in each of the lands she visited.

The Sun watched her read the words of her story as the realization of the power given to her slowly sunk in. It continued in its speech to remove any ounce of doubt Evaline could hold, "You can create combinations of words that guide your life and determine the actions that happen within it. Know I will continue to shine light as well. But this, this is your home. No boundaries. It exists wherever you are."

Tears filled Evaline's eyes as she searched for words to thank the Sun for giving her all the things she never thought she would have; things that her previous life deemed her unworthy of owning: an identity, her place in life, in this world.

"You don't have to thank me." The Sun knew her mind. "Simply live as you were called to. You know what to do now."

Evaline nodded and wrapped her fingers around the necklace that held the Stone of Imagination around her neck. Everything made sense now. She caressed the stone, thinking about the first time she saw FeFe in action. As she was taught to do, Evaline stretched out her left hand, keeping her fingers in a fist. One by one, she pointed her index, middle, and ring fingers to the blank page, shooting sprays of green, blue, and red to create a beautiful mosaic, representing her journey through the country, sky, and sea.

Focusing on the blank pages, Evaline thought about all those she wished to see again. Namaste Majie and Bookend Rasha said she would save them. And now, she understood. She could bring them and FeFe into her world, or design a new one specifically for them.

And Seahorse Cink... he would come too. Maybe as a friend, perhaps as something more. Time would tell. But for now, Evaline was on a very particular journey.

Evaline paused as she considered the people she met throughout the lands she had hoped at the time never to see again. Jenadine came to mind above all others due to their extended, relentlessly harsh conversation. Evaline actually tried- really tried- to become friends with them and help them. She was sure she could have won over the head on the right, but the left one was so much louder and fiercer. If only someone could break through to the head on the right before it disappeared because of the one on the left...

That's when Evaline knew the truth. She couldn't take the Good out of these lands. Although it would be wonderful to live in a world where only the best of everyone existed, there'd be no one who could save those that needed it the most. Bookend Rasha, Namaste Majie, FeFe, Cink- they weren't in need of saving; *they* were the rescuers, the ones that would help everyone else in each land. If Evaline took them away, there would be no one to set the example of what it means to be Good, and the hope for everyone else would fade.

Besides, without encountering those influenced by wicked motives, she never would have known just how special the friends she made actually were. And there were still so many people to meet in all the lands.

Evaline considered the terrible feelings she had when entering the World of Darkness... all those she did not understand at the time... and the ones that appeared during her journey. Hunger, anger, pain, betrayal, loneliness, heartbreak, embarrassment, regret. Even though they never felt the greatest, Evaline knew she needed those feelings. Without the lows, the highs wouldn't be as valued. A balance of good and bad was necessary to grasp the full scope of appreciation for people and experiences in life. Evaline's past made her present journey and the hope for her future much sweeter.

With the words on the wall to her left, Evaline documented the account of her past, including the feelings of darkness, as memories both painful and joyful rushed her at once, finally all returning to her mind. On the wall to her right, she created the story of a present filled with hope and love, and unlimited free space to design the future as she wished. The words did not stop flowing as the story of her heart was unveiled, bit by bit, creating her own personal masterpiece.

Evaline drifted to the white ground in-between the walls now beautifully marked with black squiggles, moved to tears at this new purpose in life. As she read the words of her story out loud, her eyelids became heavier, her excitement morphed into exhaustion. "Thank you, Sun, for finally showing me the life I was meant to live."

With that, Evaline fell into a restful, blissful sleep.

7

New Beginning

Evaline's lifts her head. The reality of the situation in front of her sinks in. The aroma of dewy grass and sap from nearby trees fills her nostrils. She's sitting outside of the car now but doesn't recall how she managed to get out. Steam is rising from the damaged, crushed hood. The cracks across the windshield are finely positioned, decorated with an otherworldly purpose. She can barely see the outline of another person, the remnants of what once was.

Evaline scans the outer windshield with her eyes, searching for the body of the lightning bug. It's no longer there. She knows why, and the truth takes her breath away. The firefly intentionally sacrificed itself for her, to turn her bad day into one of hope, to alter the course of her future with endless possibilities she never before believed in. The firefly's life ended so she could live hers again, almost for the first time, since it had been so long since true life had been breathed in her.

The melancholy tune she heard earlier begins faintly playing once again. The other fireflies are coming back. Lights swirl around her, enveloping her in their comforting embrace. This time, they came specifically for her.

They spin faster in a circle around Evaline, providing her the extra help she needs to stand up, despite the aching pain that shoots through her body. Evaline doesn't look back at the past that's sitting in the destroyed car. She only looks forward, following the fireflies as they lead her through the forest, and in her journey to the country, sky, sea, and somewhere in-between.

ABOUT THE AUTHOR

Lauren Eckhardt is an award-winning Young Adult and Women's Fiction author, who has a particular love of writing stories centered around second chances in life and the self-strengthening journeys of the characters through them. She currently lives in Illinois with her husband and two boys, happily surrounded by books.

Sign up for my newsletter to get information about new releases, giveaways, special discounts, book recommendations, events, and more!
Newsletter Sign-Up
www.AuthorLaurenEckhardt.com

If you loved this book, please consider leaving a review, which can help indie authors like me a ton and are incredibly appreciated. Thank you!

Also, be sure to connect with me on Facebook and look for the link for my special reader's group!

www.ingramcontent.com/pod-product-compliance
Lightning Source LLC
Chambersburg PA
CBHW032042180726

48284CB00008B/2714